Dear Alison (City Cuz),

Who would have thought
that I could put this
together!

love you

Mark (Country Cuz)

AKA

Fletch

07. SEP. 17

Stranded Foxes

Forthcoming Title

The Storm on the Sea of Galilee

Stranded Foxes

FLETCH MALLORY

First published in the United Kingdom in 2017 by
412 Press

First Printing

1 9 4 5 3 8 7 6 2 10

First edition

ISBN 978-1-9997930-0-5

Produced by the Choir Press

For
Susie Stones
who resides in every word

Contents

⸎

Layton

—⁓⁓—

I fully expected to die.

What I didn't expect was a black horse to canter down the High Street and trample the guy holding a gun to my head. But surreal as it might seem, that's what happened.

Three, four seconds go by and I snap out of the initial shock. I look at the twitching body of Henderson lying before me, blood leaking from the back of his head, and then look up at the backside of a rather fine looking horse. There's a blonde girl riding the horse – she says to me, 'Pick up the package, you idiot!'

'Henderson's dead,' I say. And then I hear the sirens approaching and the clatter of hooves as she vacates the scene.

'Who was that?' I think. I'm in shock, more because I was certainly dead five minutes ago, rather than any feeling for Henderson. Psychotic killer.

By the time the police arrive the paper package is in my hand but the girl is gone. I'm handcuffed and placed in the back of an unmarked car; the story of a horse and a dead body on a central London street sounds ridiculous, even to the subconscious voice in my head. But there's blood on the street, and it's not mine.

I'm being questioned. The story of a horse doesn't wash with the Inspector and to be honest, an hour later, even I don't believe it any more. Apparently there's a mixture of codeine and alcohol in my blood. Maybe I dreamt it? But no, forensics confirms it. The Inspector who sits across from me hasn't displayed any sign of humanity since I arrived. He seems genuinely disappointed when he tells me that they found horse hair on the corpse and a hoof-shaped indentation at the back of his head.

'I can go then?' I say, maybe a little too cheerily.

'I wouldn't say that, Mr. Layton.' His mouth moves but there's no hint of warmth. 'The package. Your prints are all over it. Why were you delivering it to Henderson?'

'Look, I've told you already. I never saw it before today. I picked it up ... an instinctive reaction ...'

'Are you sure,' a pause, 'you're telling the truth?'

I feel like laughing when I look into his serious eyes. I always feel like this in sober situations; funerals, job interviews, near death experiences. The laughter lurks behind my eyes but I suck it in.

'Henderson's fingerprints aren't on it,' he says to me with a slightly sarcastic edge. My pulse quickens. I can feel the sweat above my lip! I daren't wipe it away; a small action that cries GUILTY!

Without losing eye contact the Inspector drops the package on the table with a thud – brown wood absorbing the sound. I never noticed before but the paper package it is wrapped in is a newspaper; probably the *Evening Standard.*

Then with alacrity the Inspector springs off his chair with his hand inside the paper package, and pulls out a gun, pointing it straight at me! Click. I lean back violently, the chair precarious on two legs. The gun wasn't loaded and the absence of noise scares me. Now I do wipe the sweat from my lip. It runs down my back. Guilt, panic, confusion. Something.

The Inspector laughs, explosively, like he has been waiting for this release, and in that instant I see him for what he is – an overworked policeman, dead on the inside. It strikes me as kind of cruel to find humour in this way, but I let it go.

He places the gun temptingly on the table near my hand. I want to touch it, hold it closely and examine it, but I leave it; metal on wood. I know the gun but I have not seen it before.

'Browning automatic,' I say coolly, 'probably manufactured between '35 and '42.'

He stares at me blankly, laughter gone, his expressionless face absorbing the silence. Then he's up and gone, Browning in his left hand, personality hidden inside the jacket of an untailored suit.

When I am returned to my cell I realise the newspaper package is in my hand. Did I pick it up? Was it given to me? Pacing up and down, my thoughts drift. And then I see it! Beyond the black print that lingers moistly with the sweat on my fingers and onto the crumpled paper; a black horse. Even though the clarity of the image is poor and it's not looking straight at the camera, my heart joins the dots. It's got to be the same horse. I never see horses.

Two-year-old black mare for sale. Caplin. Black Rook Farm... Caplin? No obvious contact details but the message is there, I just don't know what it means.

It's 11pm before I'm brought back to the interview room. My head hurts. I need something but I'm not sure what it is. The Inspector fires questions at me from the floor; he's agitated, adjusting the tempo of his questions like the octaves of an operatic singer. Some I can't answer. Some I choose not to. We play cat and confused mouse. Is this just an act?

'Give me something, Layton,' he says, exasperated. 'You weren't just a bystander. It's not every day a gun is put to your head! We know you've had contact with Henderson before.'

'Caplin told me there's a horse for sale at Black Rook Farm.' It's the last thing I say. My final words at 11:59, before the day is through. I hold his gaze. No words pass between us, but what we do not say speaks volumes.

Five hours later and the constable on reception is handing me back my belongings. Crocodile skin wallet. Two pounds fifty in Sterling. A couple of Euros. A single peso. An unwound watch. A locker key – B257. And a brown envelope.

I get into the black London cab that waits invitingly outside the station, the brown envelope heavy in my left hand, peso in my right, cool against hot skin.

'Piccadilly Circus,' I say. The cab moves off, dodging an early morning bike messenger cutting in on the right, pink striped musette bag swinging loosely. The blonde girl at the wheel I eye, cautiously. Last time I saw her she was riding a horse.

'Why did you kill Henderson?' I say to the girl at the wheel.

'I saved your life. You're a valuable asset, Layton. You aren't just a killer like Henderson, are you?' It was a rhetorical question.

Silence sits between us, broken only by the radio, as I look at her green eyes in the cab's rear view mirror.

3

'... *entrepreneur Frank Caplin has been found dead on his family estate. A spokesperson close to the family tells of a long-term fight with cancer- an illness he struggled with despite his recent independent political activity and scathing rhetoric on the power of the media ...*'

'Frank Caplin's dead?' I ask in disbelief.

'Yes.' She looks at me closely, pulling the cab to the edge of the curb. 'You're hired, Layton,' she says.

'This is not my stop.'

'Get out. We'll be in touch.'

Henderson (deceased)

⸙

Everything is foggy.

I might be dead, but if I could remain focussed for long enough I may be able to figure out who killed me. Can ghosts have concussion? I guess anything is possible on the cusp of virtuality.

As my soul drifts from my body the first memory that comes to mind is of a beach. I can feel soft yellow sand gradually sinking beneath my white toes, hairy ankles showing from the folded rolls of my neat black suit. A silver and red splotched tie is undone from my neck and I carelessly drop the silk material into the sea and watch it briefly float in the clear water. Can salt water cleanse the deep red stains from this cleverly disguised noose? There's blood on my hands, much blood; out damned spot!

And then. I'm in a classroom reading *Macbeth* out loud to old McKlusky and the rest of 2B; 'ou- ... outtt, d- ... dd- ... dddamned spp spot!' I stutter and the class laughs silently behind shaking hands, grins barely concealed. Riley is sent out for openly laughing, but it's too late, the damage is done, the repetitious hurt is too deep. Many years later I experience minor satisfaction from smashing Riley's face to a pulp. But the emptiness and hurt were still there, lurking behind my dead eyes, even after leaving a dog-eared copy of *Macbeth* in his hands before vacating the scene. Discarded memento.

I'm back at the beach now and there's an olive-skinned senorita laying on the sandy expanse, propped up by her elbows, red bikini hiding what only my imagination can complete. Her body is beautiful, but it is her eyes I notice. She looks at me without judgement, just the idle curiosity for a man without shoes, walking in a suit on her beach. I glimpse redemption in her eyes as she calls out 'Hola!' and beckons me over with a casual wave of her hand.

I convinced myself I could hide in this reality. But I knew **they** would find me. Eventually.

I ignored my pager three times in as many months. The fourth time it sounded I threw it in the ocean, watching it plunge out of sight, letting the salt water destroy my final electronic contact. But when you fall in with the wrong people they always find you.

Time had no meaning, sea fishing off the Spanish coast. Sea bass, sole and the occasional swordfish I caught off the side of Juan's blue and white boat, *El Filosofo*. This tub was all rough splintering wood and frayed weathered rope. Lovingly unattended. In the afternoons I would sleep in the scattered shade of an olive tree, only to be woken by crabs pinching my rough-soled feet. When Anise wasn't dancing, I would lie in her arms and feel the pain of the past slowly seep away.

The pain had nearly disappeared when **they** returned. Why bring lead into a place of beauty? But they did and I wasn't clean anymore.

I left with them. You can't escape the future even when it's not yet written. I swapped frayed shorts for a snappy suit. A pistol and brown paper package awaited me as I stepped from the plane, delivered by the subtle brush past of a woman with no words, just cheap scent and cigarettes.

I finished the job assigned to me. Payment was made in another brown paper bag which I didn't even open but absentmindedly pushed through the letterbox of an unsuspecting charity shop.

Many times I thought of my beach and the girl in the red bikini, and knew I couldn't return. My anger rested with Layton because him I could reach. How dare he spoil my salvation! So I found him like only I knew how; I'm more than just a gun. When I do, we scuffle but the cards have already been dealt and there is a pain in my head.

Now from above I look down on my body and then sideways up the street at the blonde with no name and a black horse as it canters into the distance. My vision goes in and out of focus. If I die today at least I won't have to run. I'm tired of running. They would catch me anyway. The world is too small to be anonymous. It's not only God who sees everything.

Samantha J

Routine. Everybody has one in the city. Even the homeless.

Every Tuesday I follow the bike messenger but today it's different. It's 8.52 and I am in the lift already. I know he will be here between 8.53 and 8.59, late for work; alone. He's got money; designer cycle fabrics and Ray-Bans, genuine, I can tell. I get it, I really do; urban cycle messenger chic. Poser! He's missed the point. Save the money. What can't be bought must be borrowed.

This is me:

Earrings: Stolen	(the market on French Street)
Dress: Stolen	(washing line No.5 Barnaby Avenue)
Shoes: Stolen	(Girls changing room, East Street Swimming Pool)
Hair Dye (Neon Pink): Stolen	(Boots, Falmouth Street)

Everything of value I can steal. And I steal everything, except money. Money I give to the homeless, the ones who aren't savvy like me.

Samantha J is my name. You won't have heard of me. I have no profile, no previous, no identity. I am anonymous. J is for Just. Just been in your pocket and stolen your tablet. Ingenious entrepreneurial thief. Kleptomaniac? Yes. Obsessive? Slightly. Meticulous? Definitely.

8.54. I spot him walking and release the doors from hold. I don't look at him when he steps inside the elevator but I see everything.

Gold ring, 24 carat, right hand index finger; unusual.
Adidas treds; comfortable, worn.
Black Rapha musette bag, pink stripe, full.
Camera, 10x optical zoom, silver.

I'm assessing my next move when the power goes out and the lift jerks to a halt! We are somewhere between floors five and six. I know this because I was counting the floors in my head, listening to the steady whirr of unknown invisible lift mechanisms. Cogs and pulleys are brought to mind. The lights have gone out, the whirring has stopped and there's just breathing – his breathing – and strands of song lyrics floating idly but loudly inside my head.

'Damn!'

I can feel the onset of panic rising up inside me. Events are moving outside of my control. The emergency back-up light flicks on and with a mixture of rehearsed panic and genuine fear I lunge for the alarm button, knocking the camera out my lift mate's hand. (I take opportunities, even in difficult situations; stealing comes first).

'Oh sorry, I'm so sorry', I say, breathless. I carefully pick up the camera and with sleight of hand I remove the memory card and tuck it into my boot. I hand the camera back, our fingers briefly touching and for the first time in months I look directly into his green eyes.

'Hi,' he says simply. 'Are you ok?' He reads the panic in my eyes, that which is an act and the undiluted fear that hides behind it. 'The alarm's pressed, someone will be here in a minute.' A slight frown. 'Do I know you?'

'No,' I say quickly. We both still hold the camera, strangely not wanting to let go, as if without it we cannot communicate.

'I see you every day. You're the girl in the lift . . . with pink hair.'

'Yes,' I answer unimaginatively, a simple reply to the obvious statement. The surprising lightness of his voice and the friendliness of his manner disarm me and I mentally let down my guard. Something inside me is desperate to confess.

'I'm a thief,' I say almost silently, oddly with a sense of relief. To my surprise, he laughs, unusually loud and passes me the musette bag, the one with the pink stripe. He thinks I'm joking?!

'Here, I'll save you the trouble.' Still laughing. Which makes me laugh.

And then, the doors open unexpectedly. The bike man is slammed forcefully against the back of the lift by a silenced bullet. Blood fills his shirt as he breathes out his last word, 'Alici… a'. And I steal the name even before the last breath leaves his lips.

The lift isn't big enough for me to hide but I step into the corner, instinctively trying to distance myself from this explosion of calculated violence. The man with the gun reaches and takes the camera, presses the button for floor 10 and steps out, taking a brief unconcerned look at me. As he leaves I notice:

A blue (silver pinstripe) Saville Row suit.
Diamond cufflinks.
A wide brimmed hat (unusual)
… and a long-barrelled gun.

The upward elevation of the lift triggers permission for the blood to move. Never have I seen so much blood! You don't realise how dark blood is until you see so much of it. Fact. The laughing bike man is dead. Fact.

And then I vomit down my dress, three times until the entire contents have vacated my stomach. And I scream, silently inside my head. Not because of the blood or even the dead body, but because vomit fills me with fear. The doors open and I run, slipping on blood, pink-striped musette bag swinging wildly, legs unconsciously heading for the fire stairs.

I run and run, then run some more.

Two hours later I uncurl from my impenetrable foetal position, step out of the safe-haven of Mario's recycling bin and slowly make my way home, choking back tears brought on by the lingering smell of vomit.

My Name Escapes Me

I follow Jesus. You may laugh or mock me but my freedom is complete. It makes no sense and perfect sense. I am happy, at peace, content; or I was content until I met the girl, the pink haired thief who stole my gold cross. *I recall the way she smiles; the way my cross now hangs from her perfectly formed neck.*

She is distracting, dangerous maybe, but I am drawn to her. Although I try to block her from my mind she remains, her presence my constant. And there's something else; although she hasn't asked me, I know she needs my help. God told me, so I stay close. We drink tea in the café across from the church, every day between ten thirty and eleven. Without breaking my imposed silence; she talks – I listen. It seems to suit her; anyway, I like hearing her voice. It reminds me of someone. When she talks, her eyes look at me like I have never done anything wrong.

She is like clockwork. Every day she touches the locks on both doors, left then right, pauses then enters the church without stepping on the threshold. She lights a candle at 10.05 and then sits on the right-hand side of the second pew to the back. After looking back for reassurance, she says prayers from 10.10 to 10.30, at least her eyes are closed so I think she is praying. Then she says, *Hey,* and we walk to the café like every day is new and surprisingly different. *How are you? I'm fine . . .* she answers her own questions. She has never asked me why I don't speak.

I haven't spoken since the incident. Not a word. There are jumbled words in my head, I just can't give them sound. I don't know who I am or what my name is.

When I walked through the door of the church that first day, my mind was blank and I had no phone and no identification, just the clothes I stood in and a bruise on my head. The priest tells me to wait:

God will reveal all in time; the Spirit will lead you. You know, he was told in a dream that I was coming; he was told to help me and just wait. So I wait in silence, with fuzzy, out-of-focus thoughts, skirting around the hazy edges of the incident, but never going in. So for the moment, while I have no name and no home, I sleep in the cold stone vestry, wrapped in green velour curtains, and share oxygen with an abundance of spiders and the occasional carefree mouse.

When your memories have disappeared, you sleep like a baby. There is nothing to wake you. But now as I lie there watching the shadows created by the flame of a flickering candle, I can't sleep. My mind is on her. You see, she didn't turn up today and although this morning I put the worry to the back of my mind, it returns magnified as the night closes in and the remaining light fades to nothing; the subtle movement of the flame finally ceases. And then I sleep, engulfed by the darkness, my hands unconsciously reaching for a cross that no longer resides at my neck.

Stasia Mendeleev

Fontaine sent me.

'Mendeleev, get down to the Tennyson building straight away. Take the rear stairs, floor 10. Crime scene. The lift. It's jammed on floor 10. I've wired the usual payment. I've temporarily sealed the building. Don't leave any evidence. Don't be seen.'

Fontaine talks in short staccato sentences and has hung up before I even acknowledge what she has said. There is never discussion.

£1000 is not enough to do this job. The risk is great. How long before I get caught? But it does pay my way through university. I must be the only Forensic Science student with genuine experience and a healthy bank balance.

I like Fontaine. She's efficient. And dangerous. At first glance she could easily be mistaken for the average no-kids thirty-something with her floaty ponytail and tailored jacket; but underneath there is something calculating, almost devious. Deceptive baby-blue eyes and a relaxed laugh in chosen company. Succinct, cold, authoritative all other times. I don't challenge her; I just do what she says and accept the money. It's not the first time I have looked the other way; sometimes borders need to be crossed; literally and metaphorically. What is the phrase in your country? Ask no questions and I can tell you no lies. Even if you asked I couldn't tell you a single tangible fact about Fontaine, but deep down I like her. No, I respect her.

So as instructed I climb the back stairs, cautiously, eyes scanning the metal steps as I absently glove both hands and unpack sterile tweezers and swabs from a pouch on my belt, and reach for the dictaphone that lies in the deep folds of my canvas, faux military jacket. I press record on this ancient pre-digital device, briefly watching the miniature cassette whirring around methodically and start my report.

1032 hours.

Fire stairs rear access. No noticeable nieprawid?owo?ci ... er, oddities or inconsistencies as I climb the stairs until I reach floor 5. Trace evidence of blood increasing. Swabs taken carefully. Floor 10 and entry into the building itself. Heavier presence of blood and partial footprints indicative of a boot-like tread, small foots, size 5, maybe 6. A woman? ... or small man? Partial thumb print on the corridor wall near the lift stairs, sample taken. Lift doors jammed open as expected ...

'Gówno!'
I shouldn't be surprised by now, but the site of a dead body makes me nauseous. It's unprofessional. I stop recording and take a breath, inhaling and exhaling steadily until I gain my composure. Breathing now regulated. I look around guiltily. Why should I be the first on the scene? Where are the police?

Button pressed and record.

Krew ... er, blood pooling on the lift floor. (Scratch that. Rewind). White male aged around 25–30, shot in the chest. Close range, reduced spray pattern. I estimate he was shot less than 6ft away, approximately an hour ago judging from the freshness of the blood and degree of congeality. Corpse lies in the back right corner of the lift, head resting against the rear wall. Distance would suggest that the shooter stood in the doorway.

I cautiously enter the lift taking care not to contaminate the scene with my DNA. The right front corner is the only available floor space which appears to the naked eye to be free from blood. I crouch there, knees bent and with gloved hand examine the bullet hole.

Bullet hole, one. Entry wound may suggest 9mm. Corpse wears cycle jersey. Black merino fabric pushed beneath the wound. No jacket. No bag. No obvious identification on his person. Right hand thumb and index fingerprints taken.

I carefully put my hand behind his back. It's a stretch but cyclists always have zipped pockets at the back. Yes!

A silver key located in rear cycle jersey pocket. Poorly etched alpha numerics. B2 ... 5 ... 7? Key bagged.

After mentally and visually checking the scene using virtual cross grids, I am about to step out of the lift in the exact reverse way I came in (reduction of scene disturbance and DNA contamination), when I spot a single, long, straight hair on the man's sock. And then another on the lift floor. I pick them up with tweezers. I press record for the final time.

Two hairs. Location: sock of corpse; lift floor. Vialled and labelled separately.

I hold them up to the light, looking through the glass cylinders. Pink dye if I am not mistaken. Detail is everything. I look one last time at the scene. Poor guy. I wonder who he is? Did someone love him? *Żal mi twojej matki.* I am sorry for your mother.

When I leave the building I make sure no one sees me, using the skills that Fontaine taught me in my training on how to avoid and lose a tail. Forensics are not the only lectures I have attended since entering the UK.

By the time I reach the bus stop the vehicle is starting to pull away, so I hold out my hand, hopeful that the driver's human kindness has not been eroded by the sullen silence of morning passengers and the disrespectful youth your country has produced. The unspoken consequence of continued prosperity and easy credit.

To my surprise the driver stops and I rush across wet tarmac and jump on, my hand lightly brushing the translucent rain droplets sitting randomly on the bright red paintwork of the exterior cab. *Surface tension: the contractive tendency of a liquid surface which allows it to resist an external force.*

I flash my bus pass and an engaging smile to the driver.

'Cześć, Mr. Driver.'

I know you English love my accent so I throw it around with my

Polish mother's smile when I need favour. *Matka* always said that everyone who smiles is beautiful. It's true.

I sit in a seat at the front, unconcerned by the other passengers, but I smell their close dampness, all like me, caught in the showers. The sun now shines at the absence of rain; its happy brightness erasing the memory of death and I avert my dreamy unfocussed eyes from the window and look down at the face on my pass.

'Anastasia Mendeleev,' I whisper quietly with a smile on my face. A beautiful name. I am the daughter of a poet and a scientist. A degree and legality is all I need and I will be free.

I hop off near a long line of roughly sculpted hornbeams that lead up to the Campus Auditorium; wet bark and scattered birdsong behind a thick layer of traffic sounds. It seems odd carrying a bag of books alongside my tools of trade. Textbooks and pencils rubbing shoulders with scalpels, gloves and vials. Evidence.

Walking up the gothic styled steps, I nod at a few of the guys and girls loitering by the entrance. I know how to fit in even when I don't.

Despite extensive modernisation, the old building is a labrynth of dusty rooms and forgotten corridors. I make my way to the corridor that runs parallel to the staff room and face a row of dented grey-green lockers that line the wall. I reach the third locker and read the familiar name smudged across the label in red ink: Dr Edison. I insert my key; there's a knack to opening: push, twist and lift. Inside is a faded poster of Ferris Bueller. The locker is empty like it always is.

Fontaine never identified Dr Edison but he gives no lectures, no classes and curiously I have never met anyone who ever knew him. The only tenuous reference I could find was to a 'Doc Edison' in an unofficial university yearbook. Doc Edison: President of 'The Fox Club', 1995. No picture.

As instructed I deposit the bags containing the swabs of blood, the vials containing the hairs and some of the prints.

The lecture entitled 'Accurate Determination of Time of Death' is already five minutes in when I enter quietly from the side door.

... but it is repeated experience that teaches the investigator to be wary of relying on any single observation for estimating the time of death and he or she would be wise to avoid making dogmatic statements based on isolated observations ...

I take a seat and look around. Its only 70% full, probably because 30% of your students are still in bed suffering from hangovers and lack of motivation. Why do you send your *dzieci* to university? Wasted opportunities.

The lecturer is enigmatic and all eyes are forward, spellbound by his words and intriguing hand gestures. But when I look around another set of eyes is not looking forward – they are staring at me. They look at me beneath a wide brimmed hat. My thirst for knowledge briefly draws my attention back to the lecturer. When I look again he is gone. Vanished. Almost like I never saw him, like my imagination placed him there to play a trick.

More lectures followed by lunch, followed by more lectures and the uneasy feeling gradually subsides. But as I walk home I feel troubled, like I have missed something, like I forgot some piece of crucial evidence or missed a vital question in an exam. And although I should be thinking of my written report for Fontaine and the excitement of hacking into the police fingerprint database, I am bothered by thoughts of the Fox Club and disconcerting eyes beneath a wide brimmed hat.

Felis Catus

───── ❧ ─────

I walk slowly on square red tiles, up high, one paw in front of the other. The early night air is cool but clean, washed by the day's intermittent showers. I only smelt the rain. I didn't see it because I was curled up on a frayed potato sack, resting on a shelf inside my favourite shed. A shed only entered by careful manoeuvrability through the broken glass of a jagged window pane. It takes some skilled jumping and dodging, even for a lean old cat like me.

I could still hear the rain – gentle patters on the corrugated iron roof, but I ignored the sounds and went back to sleep. I didn't even open my eyes when a family of mice broke into the grain sack, but I smelt all three of them. I had already eaten. Let them gorge; fat mice taste better.

You use your eyes but for me my nose is more reliable. That's how I sensed the danger, today in the allotment shed. Midway through an exhausted yawn I caught the scent of a fox! Awake! A large red fox eyed me coldly through the damaged window, sitting casually in a tidy line of carrots, wondering whether I am lunch, whether I am worth the challenge, worth the potential pain and inconvenience of a fight. But I make myself big, my eyes fierce. The decisive survive – run or stand your ground – there is nothing in between, only indecisiveness, which leads to death or worse … mediocrity.

Back to the roof.

I sniff the air enjoying its slightly smoky scent. I am up high, three stories reached by the crisscross of makeshift ladders; moss-filled drain pipes, flat roofs and the occasional open window. This is my territory. Even Blackx, a large male on the corner of Ninth, won't come near me or dare to sit on my roof. I don't even fight well, I'm just lucky and have swagger. Anyone can improve their play book with false bravado and confidence.

Up high I see stars. Literally. They appear increasingly clear as we edge past twilight. I love the way they glitter, flickering, distant and too numerous to count; more numerous than the rough strays occupying the abandoned warehouses by the docks.

I will let you in on a secret: I use the North Star as a marker to find my way around Town; scent trails are for those of unknown heritage, and the uneducated.

I sense an irregularity some yards before arrival. The roof window is shut; Matka always leaves it slightly ajar – a whisker's width – so I can slip through, balance precariously on the ornate light fitting then jump to the kitchen table. An acrobat, Matka called me. That I am.

I see Matka through the glass; she's backed up to the table, paws at full stretch. I tap on the window with sharpened claw and select a sound, you know, the meow that sounds like a howl. Unusually she doesn't look up.

And then a man. And they are dancing, erratic steps to the side and hands to the head; but I hear no music. A loud cry and Matka crumples to the floor like a disused cloth, instantly asleep. The man retrieves the small moving window which Matka is constantly pawing, pauses, looks up at me and is gone. When he looks at me, do you know what I see in his eyes? Nothing. Absolutely nothing. And I briefly wonder why Matka, who is so happy, would be friends with this man.

I scratch and scratch at the window. Eventually it opens and I jump from light to table to floor. I lick Matka's hand, push my jowls into her face but she remains asleep. My saucer is upturned and lies near her head, her hair damp with milk and something sticky. My rough pink tongue licks up the red flecked milk from the cold stone floor. Spilt milk, nobody is crying over it, just sleeping.

Purring contentedly I move from the cold floor to the relative warmth of a discarded paper sheet which lies near Matka, and lick my sticky paws. Sitting on white paper, I look down at the random uniformity of black lines, curls and symbols. What does it say? How would I know, I'm a cat, I don't read words, just the stars which move through time, and are the same yesterday, today and tomorrow.

Elephants at Night

‒‒‒ꜱ ꜱ‒‒‒

Heat.

The humid jungle heat is oppressive as I move from the relative safety of the clearing into the tangled undergrowth. I must find a way out.

I am no more than ten metres in and my pyjamas are soaked with sweat and torn by a mnogość of thorns. Panic rises, but I hold it in until a snake slithers across my bare feet. Aaaaaahhhh! Monkeys chatter and run, birds cry out and vacate the scene and I scramble haphazardly through the dense green foliage. I am lost, no question about it; every tree looks the same, every leaf identical. I stumble in a hopeful direction, blinded by the salty sweat that runs into my eyes and the onset of panic which dissolves all logical judgement.

Then roots trap my feet and I roll head first down a concealed ravine. A flurry of green, a shot of white light, then darkness. Darkness so black and empty that I fear that my brief existence is over.

Time.

Indeterminable amounts of time have gone past and when I awake the darkness is now night. My head rests on a rock and once busy insects sway giddy from feeding on the sticky blood that runs freely down the side of my face.

I'm thirsty and bordering on delirious when I sense the movement of water and on hands and knees I crawl forward, a faint spark inside of rekindling hope.

An elephant stands before me, large and grey, with skin weathered leather, wrinkled but majestically huge in size and pattern. One eye rests on me as its long trunk drinks from the river. The moon's reflection lies on the surface, rippling deceptively from the subtle movement of the water. I remember that reflection is the change in direction of a wave front at an interface between two different media.

Deep in the river framed through the curve of the elephant's arched trunk, I see a woman wearing a white lab coat just standing there watching me. Her eyes are dark and unsmiling, which is unusual because it's my mother, and she always smiles.

'Matka?' I call out hesitantly.

Only the elephant responds, sombre grey eyes suddenly mischievous. He squirts me with water, a whole trunkful, full in the face. It washes the blood away. Instinctively I laugh; the elephant trumpets in response and gently lifts me up with hairy trunk wrapped tight and launches me into the river.

I am now approximately three metres away from my mother, almost close enough to touch but still out of reach. An uncloseable gap. She smiles briefly and then begins filling test tubes with grey-green river water. Each one is the same dirty green apart from the seventh tube, which is pink like the raspberry cordial we used to drink in Babka's garden on a hot summer's day. Matka is touching a hand-held device with a flickering screen. Fuzzy dots and distorted images. She looks at me and smiles.

'Znalazłem odpowiedź!' she says excitedly in Polish. I have found the answer! And then water that was once still rushes passed me and Matka is knocked over by the unexpected force and we are both carried downstream.

'Matka!' I scream, but as I take in water, with certainty I know she is gone.

Despair and fear creep up and pull me under, and just when the remaining oxygen in my lungs is used and I am ready to submit, I am forced to the surface and briefly spy a wide brimmed hat floating by. An unconscious signal that death has not yet spared me; it might claim me still.

After the hat, a body floats along. My father, pale and clearly dead, but with a serene smile on his face, like he is happy to be resting in this dangerous river. As always, he is holding a book. It lies neatly on his chest. It is black with silver writing on the spine, delivering the message, 'Never Give Up.'

I grab the book, clutching it hopefully, and watch the lifeless body float away. I feel an urge to open the book. The pages are wet and the ink has run; the words and letters a messy pile destined to fall off the edge of each page. But the pictures are crisp and clear; some faces I know, some I will know in the future.

Miaaoowwl!

A drowning cat struggles to stay above the water's surface and distracts me from the magnetic pull of these images. I desperately, urgently, completely want to keep hold of the book – I know it holds answers to questions not yet asked – but the cat calls to me. The cat is drowning and I hesitate for long, guilty seconds and then ditch the book and lunge for a handful of drenched fur and hold him close like a favourite teddy bear on a dark sleepless night.

Sounds.

Rushing water and the deep thunderous rumble of elephants feet crashing through the jungle. And then a long trunk lifts us to the safety of a grey, leathery back. I feel safe at this height as we walk off down the elephant jungle highway. We sit atop our rescuer for miles and miles; never have I felt as safe as I do on this night, high on the back of this majestic beast. As we journey I watch small creatures scurry carefully beneath large feet. Bright eyes view us secretly from the tree canopy.

At first it is a dot in the distance – a light shining in the darkness – and as we come closer, a fire in a clearing. The elephant sinks to his knees and cat and I slide off onto dried grass and trampled bracken, and let the fire's heat comfort our damp bodies.

Like the beat of a drum, the feet of many elephants stamp in the jungle clearing and as I look around, two dozen elephants walk in a circle around the smoky circumference of the fire. Trunk to tail, trunk to tail. Feet stamping, ears flapping, tusks shining, noses trumpeting!

On the edge of the fire I see broken glass and move closer to investigate. Test tubes, all broken bar one. The seventh tube is now empty except for a single pink hair. Beside it, almost buried by drying leaves, is mother's hand-held device. The flickering screen is now clear and the still image of a pretty girl with pink hair and serious eyes stares back at me, and the letters underneath spell the name: Samantha Just. The noisy circling elephants are now silent and watch me unwaveringly with wise, knowing eyes.

The fire continues to burn. And as I look into the hypnotic flames I see an old science teacher at the blackboard, chalk-edged words and shapes describing the fire triangle. When he moves away I see three images:

Fuel: Scattered paper sheets of chemical equations on the floor of my kitchen.
Heat: A man sleeping restlessly by the fading light of a candle.
Oxygen: A wounded girl lying on a hospital bed, receiving oxygen from a plastic mask.

The fire burns. The heat. The oppressive heat.

'Why am I stranded?' I say tearfully to myself. 'I am lost!' I shout to the emptiness of the jungle.
'No one is truly lost', says the cat beside me, absently licking a four-toed paw. 'Look at the stars, Matka. Head North and you will find your way out.'

Head North.

***

Her eyes flicker behind closed lids. Rapid eye movement as dreams form from reality and beyond.

'When do you think this fever will break, doctor?' says the nurse touching the patient's brow.

'I don't know. It's odd; she appears to have malaria and has lost a lot of blood from the wound to her head. Have you found the next of kin yet?'

'No, her ID was fake. The police are looking for the woman who called the ambulance.'

An Assassin's Descent

I am bad. Descended from pirates, the blood of thieves and looters taints my veins.

As I unscrew the silencer from my gun I glance briefly at the frightened girl with pink hair and absently slip the camera into my suit pocket, then turn and walk away from the lift. The dead bike messenger's story is finished, just as mine will be soon. If you are patient I will tell you how with certainty I know this.

Bad people with guns kill and have no remorse and as I walk down the corridor I try to fathom why I have just strayed from type and let the girl live.

When you are walking the streets, a thick trench coat is the best place to hide a long-barrelled gun. A carefully selected weapon of choice. At home I leave it on the coffee table, hiding in plain sight. Think where you shouldn't hide it and leave it there. That's what my uncle taught me, along with several techniques for picking a lock and how to dig a shallow grave. So when I am home the gun sits on the coffee table next to loosely read copies of *National Geographic* and a small pewter bowl, holding an odd mix of loose change, pot pouri and a scattering of uncut diamonds.

Yes, you heard correctly, uncut diamonds. The remains of my ancestral heritage that have not been sold, bartered or shaped into ostentatious cufflinks.

I was thirteen when my uncle first told me the story; the true story of the *Mary Celeste*. I thought it was just a fable, tall as a ship's mast, until the moment he opened up a worn leather pouch revealing a broken wooden arrow shaft and silver arrow head. The pointed silver now lies in my pocket, smoothed by the passage of time and the continual friction against the fabric inside the pocket of my Saville Row suit.

History will tell you that Olivier Devereaux, First Mate of the *Dei Gratia* was the first person to board the unmanned *Mary Celeste*, but this is an untruth; the diamonds that sit on my sleeve testify to this.

Albertine, my great-great-great uncle, an aspiring young Lieutenant aboard the naval ship *Marathon*, first saw this mysterious vessel riding listlessly upon rolling waves off the coast of Santa Maria in the Azores, and changed the course of my family line forever. No male in our family has lived past the age of forty since. Cursed! If you don't believe me, wait around a while; I was thirty-nine last year.

As the story is told, silence met Albertine as he climbed aboard the faltering vessel and instinctively loaded his musket – a small comfort against a growing sense of unease. Melting ice lay on the deck and water crystals sat in the ropes of the rigging. By the time he was making his way below deck, Devereaux had boarded and they silently nodded acknowledgement to each other but were unwilling to speak, as if to break silence would unleash all the fury of a sailor's imaginatious superstitions.

There was an eerie quietness about the boat; an ethereal, chilling stillness in the air as if all the wind and heat had been purposely re-moved. Albertine saw undisguised fear in Devereaux's eyes and knew they reflected his own. They cautiously moved below deck. Contrary to historical records, the *Mary Celeste* was not unmanned, but in the galley around a long oak table sat the twelve crew, in front of roasted chicken, once crusty bread and tankards of half-empty rum. Each man was dead, or were they frozen? They were all grey and cold, with frost in their hair. Yes, twelve frozen men. It was the thirteenth man who shocked Albertine, with his wide, blue eyes and braided blonde hair. He was not frozen but was clearly dead with a silver arrow through his heart and tight fists laying to rest on the galley table.

Albertine felt nauseous and to escape from the uncanny scene he entered the Captain's cabin. Strewn disorderly on a rich, oak desk lay an assortment of maps and sea charts; and a brass-encased compass which spun continually at speed, anti-clockwise, like a whirlpool on a stormy night. Strangely the clock above the desk was upside down and Albertine wondered what strange fate befell this ship and crew. The final entries of the Captain's log book read like this:

13th December 1872

We passed a school of dolphins on a cold but sunny day off the coast of the Azores. There was something odd about them. They were less playful than usual and were moving North. I sensed their urgency. I have never seen so many together. Within half an hour the sun had disappeared and a winter storm descended on us as quick as a brown hare being chased by a hungry fox. Wind, lightening, hail and even snow claimed the night with a fury so intense that I thought we would not survive with our vessel intact! The compass stopped working! Round and round it spun, relentless, like a sycamore seed released from its tree.

14th December 1872

The storm has passed and the ship is intact apart from the lifeboat, whose ropes broke in the night. We watched it sail off into the dark expanse of the Atlantic.
Today is a day distastefully without sun, and the sea as thin and muted of colour as the vegetable soup served up by our cook. We picked up the stranger on a makeshift raft, which appeared to be a large, white door. I can only describe him as odd and he spoke a tongue that neither I nor my crew could ascertain its origin. Not even the Doctor, who has claimed to have travelled to the Americas and beyond, could place it. He was clearly scared, and for this I am wary but the good Lord clearly tells us that everyone is our neighbour, so I bring him on board despite the crew's superstitious misgivings.
Note: the stranger appeared to have no possessions apart from the clothes he stood in and a timepiece strapped to his wrist. I have heard of these but this was truly odd; it had no hands and its numbers flashed! I will endeavour to investigate further tomorrow when he is more at ease.

Crew still nervous about cargo. Compass broken.
Young Tom's 'sea dog' still nervous; I locked him below deck.

When Albertine finished reading, he heard a gasp from the galley and ran back to see a wide-eyed Devereaux, gazing at diamonds sitting in the prised-open hand of the thirteenth man. They glittered enticingly, shining brightly like a thousand twinkling stars in stark contrast to the frozen greyness of the galley.

'There's more in his pockets,' Devereaux exclaimed excitedly.

Albertine moved towards him with haste and changed my family's future with a single action, exchanging long life for the trappings of wealth and clock watching.

At this point my uncle's story changed several times during retelling, depending on whether he was sober or intoxicated. 'Yes, my boy, Albertine slipped on the icy deck and his musket inadvertently fired. Yes, my son, Devereaux's heart gave out at the immensity of wealth before him.' But deep down I knew Albertine killed Devereaux in cold blood; I sense it every time I touch the diamonds.

Little else is known of this story except that the crew's cargo exploded and the remains of the ship sank in the ocean. The only reported survivor a scraggy, curly-haired dog.

That story changed my life. It changed my great-great-great uncle's life. It made him wealthy beyond his imagination or class status, but it was quickly spent on whores, gambling and honest business ventures which required brains and not money. Among all the men in my family, only I have succeeded. I have been wealthy. I am wealthy. But with just days remaining before my fortieth birthday, my time is running out and you can't buy time, can you.

The side street that I walk down is deserted when I come across the pregnant woman.

Compassion. I wasn't born with it and I certainly didn't inherit it. But now I feel it inside of me as I watch the woman with two hands on the wall and head bowed, cry out in pain. This is weakness in my world. What use is compassion? But I can't let go of this tugging feeling as I hear her heavy, painful breath.

'Help me,' she wheezes out.

I look her in the eye and briefly share her pain, which is a mistake on many levels, not least because I will be late for the drop off.

Reluctantly I move forward and she grips my hand so tightly and with such ferocity that I am surprised because she is slight of frame despite her pregnant state.

'Help me.'

The simplicity of her request stops my heart. I don't help people; I don't care. I don't get into people's lives. But when she asks me the third time with tears in her eyes, I know I will. A day of firsts?

'Please help me.'

And I lead her to my car and cushion her carefully, with a gentleness I didn't know I possessed. Safely positioned into clean, leather upholstery, I run around to the driver's side and start the engine, unconsciously trying to map out the quickest route to the hospital in my head. I then realise I haven't even spoken to her.

'Er ... you ok?' I say. She doesn't answer; her eyes are fixed on the handle of the gun as it peeks guiltily out of my rain coat.

Danny (Corporal)

I had a dream. The colours and essence of it were so vivid that it was a relief to find I was still alive when I woke up. But the images hung there, clear though out of reach, like a mirage in a desert. It was an extraordinary dream because I was with grandad and grandad hasn't been 'with us' for a number of years. Grandad has dementia; he doesn't know who I am. He calls me 'Corporal' and asks me if 'the chaps are ready' every time I visit, which isn't often because, as mum says, I'm a teenager and lazy and to be honest, what do you say to somebody who can't remember who you are?

Closing sleepy, flickering eyelids I try to return; to climb inside the dream and re-live it. Good dreams, exciting dreams, are clear and memorable and pull you back in with invisible rope. And I am back in a grassy field surrounded by trees. I watch a tall man with tired, serious eyes scan the horizon. It's Normandy 1944. Although this stranger is young and good looking, with tight skin and a finely trimmed moustache, it is clear to me that Lieutenant Blackwood is my grandad. The sepia photo on Nanna's mantelpiece lays claim to this.

A splintered, upturned ammo crate is utilised as a makeshift table and my grandad spreads out a map of Normandy with dog-eared corners and hand-pencilled notes in the margin. A small group of dishevelled, khaki-clad soldiers with dirty but determined faces gather around, and I am proud to see grandad detail an attack plan to liberate a village west of St-Lo. He winks at me, mouths some co-ordinates and we're off, Lee Enfield at the ready and grenades hanging loosely from belts and ammo straps. We're through a break in the bocage at a steady pace, spread out thinly and keeping low in long, unkempt grass. A scattering of farmhouses are sighted and it is not long before shots are fired. Running. I see two men taken down to my left but I reach the safety of the grey stone wall with grandad leading the way, brandishing a Browning Automatic. Staccato gun fire surrounds me and rubble from an exploding wall hits my face as a German half-track unloads a shell. Courageously, two soldiers run at it in seemingly erratic zigzags and empty magazines and grenades until it is silenced. Smoke drifts. A French peasant boy runs through the field. Thirty, maybe forty minutes elapse and the pace of the scene begins to slow, punctuated by the occasional gun shot and the sound of flames consuming the burning vehicle.

Then it is me and grandad, side by side next to a concrete pillbox that appears disused.

'Clean it up Corporal,' he says.

I look down dark steps and then throw a grenade to be sure, but it is thrown back out! I watch it bounce on the concrete before me. A snap detonation then boom! Followed by silence; sound ceased; blood from my ears and explosive light. A hot stickiness runs down the back of my neck. I fall.

As the smoke clears and the numerous dust particles catch the light, I hear a tiny flutter of wings and then all is finally silent.

When I awake all I can visualise are the map coordinates that Lieutenant Blackwood, my grandad, gave me. So I write them down on a scrap of paper and mum's surprised when I ask if I can visit grandad with her today, and we do. I drive my rusting Vauxhall Nova, with my nervous mother in the passenger seat and 'L' plates tightly attached to bumpers with white string.

'Hi Joan,' grandad says to my mum from the midst of a mustard toned sofa. I see the pain these words cause hiding discreetly in the depths of mum's green eyes. It sits there hurting and absent of comfort. My mum's name is Ann.

'Ah, Corporal, are the chaps ready?'

'Yes, Lieutenant Blackwood,' I say. Mum stares at me funny. Grandad looks me in the eye. There's a pause.

'Good,' he says. 'Today we will need courage and not everyone will make it back, so make sure the lads have a good breakfast.'

'Yes sir.' The words are clear, his eyes have clarity and regained some of their sparkle.

Ann walks to the shops because Joan makes her miserable. When she's gone I apprehensively place the scrap of paper with the inked coordinates on the table next to grandad's coffee.

'Danny,' he says, 'where did you get these?'

Danny?

'Headquarters,' I say.

'Straight from the top?'

'Yes sir.'

'Quick, get out my maps, Corporal.' There's an urgency in his voice, a directness, a clarity and authority which I haven't heard before and I am hooked, I am in, and there is nothing that will tear me away from this path.

Grandad says the maps are in the attic in a mahogany chest. And when I haul it down from creaking steps and wipe away layers upon layers of dust, I find the name William R. Blackwood engraved next to the brass lock. Surprisingly the key to entry resides loosely around grandad's wrinkled neck, beneath a pointed, beige striped collar.

'Why haven't you shown me this before?' I say, almost accusingly as I uncover a German luger from the confines of a Nazi flag.

'Careful, that's still loaded,' he says in response.

The chest's contents amaze me; five medals, a brass compass, a silk escape map, the stub of a cigar and a green cloth patch depicting a snarling fox, with its tail protecting the number ten. The maps lay beneath these treasures and grandad grabs them hastily and spreads one across the veneer of his 1970s coffee table. To my surprise the neat grids do not box in parts of Normandy but the south coast of England.

'Here,' he says, pointing a finger. 'I remember now, close to Southwick House. Churchill loved Portsmouth. Let's go.'

I haven't managed to acquire a full license and I am not sure whether grandad has got hold of all his faculties to make this legal, but we drive off hastily in my rusting blue Nova with grandad riding shotgun, after a hurried note to 'Joan' left on the table next to a fraying Nazi flag.

Running on empty the petrol gauge has been showing less than zero for the last ten miles, but grandad insisted there was no time for delay, and field after field and track after track eventually cease when grandad declares, 'We are here'. He takes one last glance at the map and then points to a copse of trees on a hill maybe a mile away.

'What's over there, grandad?'

'Corporal, are the chaps ready?' I look at him and the clarity in his eyes has gone.

'Wait here, grandad,' I say softly. I get out the car, apprehensively sweeping the perimeter with untrained eyes and after one backward glance, climb the barbed-wire fence bordering a track lined with an assortment of beech and ash.

The sun is warm on my neck and the grass is long and wild, dotted with flowers and bees and nettles and insects. I feel uncomfortable leaving grandad in the car but we have reached this far and there is no turning back now.

Twigs and forgotten leaves snap and crunch under foot as I enter the copse, and despite the cooling breeze and warmth of the sun, a peculiar feeling makes me wish I had brought the luger. Then I see it – a concrete bunker, like the pillbox in my dream, sits wedged between trees and a gathering of brambles and tiny withered blackberries.

Moving cautiously forward my eyes see the trip wire lining the bunker before my brain can engage and force my feet to stop. A loud noise, an explosive flash of light and I am thrown to the ground with torn denim and blood leaking from my head and legs. Hearing lost, I hold my ears and in slow motion I see a large grenade-shaped pine cone bounce on the aged concrete and watch disturbed dust glittering in the air, caught by the sun. And then as my head finally rests on the dry, leafy floor I watch a butterfly flutter, then land on my hand, flecked with patches of sun and dappled shade. And these are the last colours I see; the black, white and red of the butterfly's delicate wings, before my remaining consciousness ebbs away and is drawn to the light.

Drawn to the Light.

Lieutenant Blackwood

※ ⌑ ※

88mm shells fire continuously. Drifting smoke.

The commandeered truck was a big target, so as a shell exploded ten yards to our right it was more than an surprise to be taken out of action by a black horse crashing through the windscreen. Broken glass, blood and horse saliva were mingled with expletives from Privates Dean and Baker, located in the seats beside me. I shoot the mare in the head, out of kindness really; but I felt relief because there is little more sinister than the panicked eyes of a frantic, dying horse.

As we alight from the vehicle shots are being fired and we crawl on our bellies through long-stemmed grass towards a Willy's jeep, crashed into the trunk of a large tree. And there in the passenger seat is none other than Winston Churchill in a thick woollen coat and peaked hat, smoking the dying remains of a Cuban cigar.

'Blasted Jerries!' he says. And I jump on him with some force because he is giant in both stature and personality; it's an instinctive but entirely necessary action because machine gun fire rakes the grass beside us and I take a bullet to the shoulder. The pain is a slight relief because I may need some physical evidence to back up this Prime Ministerial assault during Court Marshall!

'Sorry sir.' The words seem absurd but a necessity – it is Churchill, after all.

With a mouthful of dirt, he looks me directly in the eye. He is clearly shaken, but he has seen battle; it runs deep within his blood. I know he is thinking of a plan because fear doesn't rest on his face, just a knowing grin and a wrinkled smile.

'I thought they had cleared this side of St-Lo!'

'So did I, sir. There appears to be a pocket of krauts over in the woods. There's an FFI dropzone to the south-west.' Then on cue, Saunier with his greying, curled moustache and Delphine, with her flamboyant red neckerchief, arrive, firing Sten guns from the hip, just as our truck blows up.

'Forces of the French Interior, sir,' I say, with slightly raised eyebrows.

'Bonjour!' he says, with his distinctly upper class British accent, and lights a new cigar. Delphine looks at Saunier in disbelief.

'Winston Churchill?! C'est incredible!'

'Bonjour, Monsieur Churchill. Frederick Saunier at your service,' he says, sticking out a dirt-encrusted hand in introduction.

'Saunier, I am outside of my comfort zone here, any ideas?'

I interrupt. 'Sir, there's the remains of a barn with a caved-in roof, just past the bend in the road. We could hole up there until back up arrives. If back up arrives.'

'It will. Saunier, any better plan?'

'Non, this is a good suggestion. Remnants of the 82nd Airborne are moving quickly through from the west. They could be here within the hour.'

On hands and knees we follow Delphine, weaving through the long grass, occasional stray bullets scattering overhead. Churchill's aide, Mattingly-Browne, unconscious from a bump to the head, is being dragged by a reluctant Private Dean who insists that, 'The corpse is most likely dead' and is certain that Churchill, 'Must 'av another driver.'

But they were Dean's last words. Baker's words were, 'Got my lucky rabbit's foot, sir', as he grinned at the Prime Minister. A bullet to the neck and heart; punctured lungs and final breath. The torrent of gunfire was merciless and unforgiving as I watched the remaining members of my company cut down before me. No amount of rabbit's feet or tightly crossed fingers can withstand the probability of death – day after day in the field, and bullet after bullet in confined forest spaces.

We are hemmed in by trees and a shallow dirt ridge, and I empty magazines at barely concealed, grey fabric ghosts. Blank, shocked faces. Bodies falling. Falling. Falling. I bring death instinctively, my conscience hidden in the unopened letters that lay in the depths of my rucksack, alongside Mother's Bible and treasured tins of bully beef, scrounged from F Company corpses. Those dead were cold and stiff, almost inhuman. Not like Dean and Baker, whose blood remained hot, whilst souls drifted upward. Did Baker know the God in Mother's book? What was Baker's first name? Private.

A fat, reassuring hand rests on my arm and I realise the magazine is empty. They are all empty; the ammunition is spent.

'That's enough, son.' I look into Churchill's baby face. When did he have time to light another cigar?

'Never give in,' I say.

He smiles. 'Never, never! We can fight another day, another hour.'

I watch Delphine tenderly touch Saunier's moustache and then close his eyes with gentle, respectful fingers. Mattingly-Browne has woken up and is sick. He removes rounded spectacles with cracked lenses and surveys the scene.

The Colonel who captured us is decorated but dishevelled and was clearly wounded underneath a charred jacket. No hat, bald, unsmiling and with a faint aroma of death cheated.

There is fresh milk in the farmhouse but no farmers. The stove is hot with half-baked bread, but no bakers. The scene is almost comfortable as Delphine, Mattingly and I sit around a rough wooden table on mismatched chairs, with Churchill at the head. The Colonel sits opposite, with a milk moustache, head back laughing, despite the obvious pain he is in. Yes, comfortable, except for the casual flick of a well-oiled luger and two young SS officers, standing erect in black coats and remorseless, gloved hands.

'You can't beat drinking milk fresh from a cow,' Churchill says.

The Colonel laughs, 'Maybe with a tot of whiskey in it!'

'Quite!'

No one else is laughing. Churchill and the Colonel act like they have known each other for years. Delphine's eyes are steel. If she were closer I am sure she would attempt to kill him with her hair grip or her young, ring-less fingers. Spontaneous courage fuelled by hatred and determination; patriotism. The krauts sense this; Delphine is the only member of this breakfast club who has hands tied. But to be realistic, I can now barely move my arm and Mattingly doesn't appear to have the stomach to fight.

'. . . yes, I suppose these are reasons for killing Franz Ferdinand, but you have to search much further back to truly pinpoint the origin of the Great War.'

I listen drowsily. The political history and origins of the Great War always confused me and explanations changed or mutated every year I attended school. I just know that my father died on the Somme in wet mud, surrounded by dead trees whilst yellow gas floated by, searching the depths of craters for gallant men with rotting feet.

As my consciousness fluctuated from loss of blood and the heat from the stove, I only half listened to the chatter batted back and forth between like-minded intellectuals. Conversation about European politics and the merits of Mozart over Beethoven littered with laughter and scattered rings of expensive cigar smoke.

Conversation stops abruptly. The Colonel is up, out of his chair, with the casually gesticulated luger now pointed directly at Churchill. His once smile-creased face now momentarily blank; then two shots are fired in quick succession and the SS officers are instantly dead. The Colonel lays the gun on the table, finishes his milk, salutes Churchill whilst standing to attention, and strides confidently out the kitchen door. When I looked through the dirt smudged glass, framed by paint-flaked wood, I see the backs of worn-out soldiers walking away from the farmhouse in tired but disciplined rigidity, following a leader with a cleared conscience. The Colonel without a hat.

'Pleasant chap. Close call, eh Lieutenant?' Churchill says in classic understatement, picking up the luger and passing it my way.

Stone the crows, I think.

Now weapons are superfluous and the vomiting has ceased, Mattingly-Browne takes charge, commandeering a passing jeep to take us back to the beaches.

Prisoners; long lines of dirty dejected faces are being processed by MPs with pressed uniforms and tight-lipped smiles. I watch a photograph taken of a German officer being searched; a stern face; and the brainwashed, unrepentant eyes of the master race. Then raucous laughter and, 'Hey, Mr Churchill.' An American twang from a bearded man with a casual half-hearted salute.

'Ruddy loud-mouthed Americans!' Churchill mutters under his breath. 'Good job Dwight's got some manners, Mattingly.'

'That's Hemingway, sir, and the Hungarian photographer, Capa. Apparently he came in on the beaches, shooting the invasion.'

'Without a gun?'

'Yes, sir.'

'With his camera?'

'Yes, sir.'

'Taking photos?'

'Yes, sir.'

'Bloody fool!'

Before he returned to Blighty, the Prime Minister said he could do with a man like me and gave me a cloth patch depicting a snarling fox with his tail curled around the number ten. Mr. Churchill shook my hand. *My hand.* Proudest day of my life. And that wasn't the last time I saw him.

I Silently Mouthed Goodbye

—&—

Thirty-nine steps led me to them. It was unintentional, unplanned.

I ascended cautiously and reached the platform to board the train without a ticket. I don't buy tickets.

That was nearly three years ago now; I remember it clearly. The 15:55; a dry Thursday in August. There were a couple of seagulls fighting hungrily over a blackened chunk of bread on the dirty concrete step. My memory is exceptional; it has always been like this.

I let six trains go past me that day before I could bring myself to step between the gap. I finally stepped across on the seventh, left foot first. Always left foot first. Unwashed people with dirty hands ride trains and buses, so I avoid them where possible. But the stealing is good; smart phones, wallets, tablets, an occasional soft toy.

If I recall correctly, which I do, that day I wore long, sparkly socks over my jeans, despite the hot weather, and white cotton gloves and Oakley's 'borrowed' from the new girl on floor one, who has money and style but no substance or sense. A pink, silk scarf, a softer shade than my hair, sat around my neck as I entered the carriage doors apprehensively. I wore it like a mask to filter out other people's uncleanness. Why do people feel the need to exhale so much?

In the carriage, rows of empty, expressionless faces sat isolated from each other by a myriad of different beats, assaulting every ear through twin wires, with faceless messages appearing sporadically on scrolling digital screens. Technology separates, stops us being truly human.

Three boys in black blazers with red trim and Latin-laced badges are unaware of the wall of self-imposed silence sitting beside them. They casually talk about *Dr Who* and unusual hair styles whilst lunging wildly and punching each other with the playful hands of schoolboy comradery.

But these bodies were just the backdrop to that particular moment in time. At the centre, the couple stood, so closely, so consumed by the presence of the other it was difficult for me to look away. I was fascinated, watching them through darkened lenses, completely distracted from the task at hand. The man. The woman. So close, almost touching, face to face with eyes searching, then fingertips unconsciously brushing. Acceptance of every imperfection of feature and character. I was transfixed. How was it possible that two people could like each other so much? How could they breathe so closely and be content?

When I saw them I knew. I instinctively knew the couple were who I had unconsciously been searching for. I felt it deep inside of me. Later, when I recovered from my decision and the events that followed, it was this inner feeling that prompted me to walk into the church.

I remember touching, skin on skin, but it wasn't like the un-awkward closeness that stood before me. It was saliva and forced intake of breath with a thousand germs, tainting. The shower later did not make me clean; the salty tears did not wash my face. Not that night or any night.

The couple hand in hand, I followed from a distance, catching handfuls of laughter and feel-good words as they drifted lightly on a subtle breeze. Littered pavements progressed to uniform trees and rust-free railings, standing proudly outside beautiful Victorian terraces. I watched them enter through a glossy red door as one, and I silently mouthed goodbye.

After that first day I returned many times, watching the searching fingers and smiling eyes. On the fourth visit I broke in and after removing street-dirtied kicks, taking care not to touch the soles, I slid in socked feet along polished oak floorboards and counted the brass screws holding them tightly in place. In the house this is what I found:

Smiling faces on photos (honeymoon on the Amalfi Coast)
A jewel-encrusted eternity ring (diamonds?)
Bank statements (£6453.77 in credit)

Multiple ISAs (Total content: £71,344.16)
A Richard Pargeter painting (bright sunflowers on green fields)
Cosy sheets (crisp and white with mauve alliums)
Rows of teddy bears! (resting quietly on the spare room bed)
A photo of a man with grey hair (Arthur Conrad Hathaway receiving a prize for architecture in '84)

In the bathroom bin:

A champagne cork
A half-eaten strawberry
Tissues (mascara stained)
A pregnancy test kit (negative)

I broke in four times and never stole a single thing. One morning I slept in their bed. The fifth time I left them my most precious gift: a small bundle, softly wrapped, in a straw basket.

When I left her in the hallway that Christmas Eve, my baby was content, asleep and beautiful. So beautiful. Most people would have called the police. They never did. I knew they wouldn't. They are not most people.

I silently mouthed goodbye.

I named my daughter ... it doesn't matter what I named her! Penny and Stephen called her Amelia. Don't judge me! I can't look after her. I'm a thief, not a mother! And she kept being sick! When I fed her she kept being sick! It scared me. It scares me. I could barely touch her or smell her. I love her. Don't judge me; I love her, damn it! But she's better off without me. Without someone like me.

***

Sometimes I watch Amelia in the park with Penny. On a see-saw, or crunching through piles of windswept leaves stacked up beside park fences. She wears red wellies, a blue raincoat and hand-knitted mittens. She likes the sun and the rain and the snow. Even the wind catches her attention. And birds and dogs and flying helicopter seeds. When I watch her laugh with creased eyes and a wide open mouth, I smile. Rosy cheeks.

Sometimes I cry; silent tears through smiling eyes. Later, on the bus, I sob into gloved hands while the real mothers, with wipes and dummies and snacks in plastic boxes look, but don't touch. I can't be touched.

Amelia's birthday is January 13th. Anonymously I send her cards; bright pictures of happy elephants or a funny mouse, once a fox with a long bristly tail. In the card: I love you. I need to write these words. One year I wrote the words: *You're a shining star, bright on a cold night.*

***

I have a routine. Today is Tuesday so I walk to the church to see the silent man, the man with no name. I like talking to him – he is clean. His silence is reassuring. He is troubled but he is at peace. The tea soothes me, his presence comforts me. He is my only friend. Tea tastes better with him.

Arthur Conrad Hathaway
1928 – 2014

The middle child of a family of seven, Arthur learned to draw when copying war-time cartoons sketched by his father, who encouraged creativity and taught him perspective. However, the heroic death of his father during the attack on the Merville Battery in the early hours preceding D-Day (for which he achieved the Victoria Cross posthumously), saw a brief spell of artistic lethargy. In an interview in 1984, Hathaway described this period of his life as 'a dark place which was damned hard to escape from'. But escape he did. These post-war years saw him begin his love for construction during the rebuilding of bombed areas of central London, under the guidance of his uncle, who taught him the family trade: bricklaying. His potential as an architect first came to the fore when his uncle's construction firm, Hathaway & McElroy, expanded in the '50s. Funded by his uncle, William 'Wild Bill' Hathaway, Arthur attended the prestigious McGill' School of Architecture, where he befriended the world proclaimed architect, Lloyd Roach. It was a friendship that lasted a lifetime through written correspondence; Hathaway's intense fear of flying left him bound to the UK, whereas Roach emigrated to Europe and finally America.

Hathaway's career and profile flourished, as did the buildings he designed. His flair for introducing a distinctly new feel to the satisfying comfort of traditional designs saw him increase in popularity among the general public and political upper classes. Hathaway was far ahead of his time when discussing and utilising sustainability within his projects, and was extremely concerned over material wastage and the legacy we were passing on to our children. Children that Hathaway had already begun to describe as: those that had forgotten the price of freedom.

It was an early meeting with Edith Pritchard, distantly related to Sir Winston Churchill, which led too much of his networking, success and more adventurous commissions. Long overdue, he eventually won the Pritzker Architecture Prize for his nature-inspired *The Green*, in 1987. Although Hathaway claimed never to have met Churchill, rumours circulated that Hathaway's ability to design in concrete like his German counterparts, his matchless integrity and spontaneous ingenuity, linked him to a rumoured Prime Ministerial bunker built at an undisclosed location.

Godfather to the daughter of his long-standing friend, surgeon and MP, Sir Michael Fontaine, Hathaway outlived his wife Evelyn, but is survived by his children, Grace and Richard, and grandchildren, Stephen, William, Beatrice and Bethany.

Although happy to talk to the press about his latest designs and views on current architecture, he did not often speak of his private life, always deflecting more personal questions back to his works. However, after his wife's death in '91, he was asked about the secrets of his long and happy marriage to Evelyn Chase-Gillespie. He replied: 'My good father taught me Ephesians 5:28. Made me learn it. *He who loves his wife loves himself.* I had a good marriage; I discovered what said 'I love you' to Evelyn and never gave up loving her. She loved words and touch.'

Amelia

—⁓—

Like a flicking of a switch, life can be extinguished. The time it takes to count to one.

When your children are small you arise early. There is no choice. They are alive, brand new and have no sense of time. They are excited by being awake. They are not burdened by the hands of a clock.

Although the beginning of the day was sunny and dry, Amelia had her wellies on as she stood by her mother's bed at 5.35 that morning. Red wellies with white spots, a blue dressing gown with ladybird buttons, and rosy cheeks framed by bobbed hair. Her hand was patting the duvet.

'Wake up, mummy. Wake up!'

By 6.30 they were all eating breakfast. Toast and jam. Strawberry for Penny and Stephen. Marmalade for Amelia. Small, sticky marmalade prints on a glass, quickly emptied of orange juice. She ran up the wooden stairs to brush her teeth and change into her t-shirt because daddy said dressing gowns aren't good for the park unless you pretend they are a coat, and hers was too fluffy and soft. Silly daddy!

By 7.10, Penny and Stephen were walking arm in arm along quiet, tree-lined streets approaching the Victorian railings and grand, stone arches that frame the park's south entrance. Stephen laughed at Amelia skipping ahead in red boots with shorts and white stick legs, and a pink t-shirt with a sparkly butterfly motif. 'Papillon,' she said, and he was surprised at her, like he was always surprised at the little things she said or did.

At 7.11 Stephen kisses Penny on the lips whilst Amelia, still ahead, stands gazing up at the lion that guards the gate, and then runs through, roaring. Aslan, she thinks.

At 7.12 Stephen and Penny were dead, hit by a car that was swerving, not speeding. It was not a painful death, just shocking and quick and final. When the car tumbled over, the boot snapped open and bags of colourful paper squares were thrown in the air, caught by a breeze and fluttered down like tickertape at a cup final. The driver crawled on hands and knees from the inverted vehicle and cried out. Anguish. He looked down at the crumpled bodies of two young lovers and ran away down the quiet street. Escape.

***

Amelia roars like a lion and runs past white climbing dog roses to an expanse of lush green grass, and chases seeds that drift on a breeze; balls of uniform fluff detached from dandelion clocks.

When she reaches the play park, Poddy is there, hiding in a yellow house with a circle for a door and a green roof. He jumps out and they roll around in the bark chippings, laughing.

'There you are!' she says happily.

The swings make Poddy nervous so he waits, watching Amelia with attentive brown eyes. He loves the slide though and they run round and round, climbing red steps, sliding down. Woosh! Climb, slide, climb, slide.

'We must have been on that a hundred times!' she says.

Amelia follows a couple of chirping red and yellow finches across the grass, with Poddy close behind, until they get to a low flint wall that separates the park from the church. On the wall: moss and a family of woodlice.

Amelia looks back at the park for mummy and daddy, slightly concerned.

'Where are they?' But Poddy is with her, so she smiles and on the third attempt they are up on the wall, high like an explorer reaching a mountain peak.

'Good climbing, Poddy.'

On the other side of the wall is the church, with its rippled glass and flint stone construction, and small trees softening an assortment of weathered grave stones next to new and old flowers. The old flowers look sad but the tight-clipped grass is happy with confetti. Leaning next to a large headstone stood a boy with a blackened face and an unusual brush.

45

'What are you?' Amelia said to the boy.

'I'm a lucky chimney sweep. Don't get too close! You'll get soot on yer clothes like me.'

'What's soot?'

'It's this black stuff innit! Don't you go to school?'

'No.'

'Who were you talking to over by the wall?'

'Poddy Flower.'

'Who?'

'Poddy Flower.'

'That's a silly name.'

'S'not.'

'Is too.'

'What's your name, then?'

'You can call me Lucky. That's what dad says I am. Where's Poddy now?'

'Sitting behind you, Lucky. And he's got a feather in his mouth and his paws are muddy!' And she hurried off with a mis-timed skip, chuckling to herself.

Lucky looked and looked but there was nobody there with Amelia. Nothing, just blades of grass and a scattering of daisies, socialising with a pair of bees. Blimey, she's got an invisible dog, he thought. Now that is lucky! And he walked off along the grey stone wall.

She didn't know how to tell the time; she just felt hungry and tired and if it hadn't been for Poddy Flower she would have cried.

'Where is mummy?' Poddy just barked loudly and wagged his tail happily and ran off. And Amelia ran after him because Poddy always knew where to go. She was surprised when he got into the rear passenger seat of the black car, but there was a tartan blanket in the foot well so they crawled underneath with tired, drooping eyes and Poddy's head resting in the circle of a wide brimmed hat.

When the wheels started to move they were both already fast asleep. Amelia dreamt of fluffy clouds and bright stars on a cold night, and the boy with a sooty face. Poddy dreamt of butterflies and bones. And as the car drove off, a sea of dandelion seeds casually floated by, travelling lazily on a sun-warmed breeze.

VW Golf (1998)

⁓ e ◦ ⁓

I feel the rust eating away at me. Under the arches; the edge of doors. This cancer would worry me if I had not lived, had not seen it all. Winding drives in the country with windows wide open, wasting a full tank on no destination, just the freedom of tarmac lined by grass hedges. I've been bumper to bumper with the beautiful models in the Kensington Streets, with shiny, pretentious owners who value objects over life. Once I raced a red Maserati down a narrow street and won; there is much pride in small achievements. I even visited Europe and topped 120 on the autobahn; the thrill of speed caught me unawares. But that was my yesterday and now I am old and worn and have a sense of finality.

I sense the presence of the man as soon as he touches me. His fingers slight and careful, like everything is special. He opens my boot, moving a jack and spider to make space for brown cardboard boxes brimming with loose postage stamps. There are all kinds in there; every colour and pattern and country. What he would want with them I do not know. He hums a tune that I have heard on the radio; he is happy, I sense this when he sits in my seat and turns the ignition. His heart beats joyfully. I feel his emotions in the leather upholstery – I sense it in the fluidity of the steering wheel.

Mileage sits on me heavy with time, but I spark up instantly.

If he knew what I knew he would not drive me. MOTs can be bought as easily as stolen passports or dope from the shadowed faces in disused parking lots. Everything is for sale. In my last diagnostic I found the following:

Oil leaks x2.
Front brake pads worn to the point of failure.
Handbrake inconsistent.
Driver's side indicator bulb missing.

Driver's seat belt faulty.
Off side rear tyre inflated well below recommended pressure.
Off side and near side front tyres illegal.
Speedometer erratic.

It's a shame that the man is so happy, because what happens next will hurt him deeply and destroy me. But there are things you can't change. Storms you have to go through. I once heard a passenger say that life sifts a man, shows him what he is made of. Some break; some rise up and fight, some stay in neutral and drift until they are dead.

The early morning is beautiful with the sun shining. It's easy for me to overheat but I try my hardest not to because me and the man have enough problems and he doesn't even know it. The radio is off but he still hums that tune; classical violins mixed with an overriding beat. Mozart's House?

The park comes into view and as we pass the noisy blue Nova I know this is the end. The speedometer is faulty I want to shout. The speedometer is faulty! We reach 45mph as we turn adjacent to the southern gate. And as I instinctively swerve to miss a curly haired dog, I have lost complete control of brakes and tyres and I feel the happiness of the man displaced by sheer horror, as my body flips over and over and crashes into two people who walk hand in hand along the avenue. The man scrambles frantically to control the steering wheel but it slips through his fingers like sand in a sieve.

I am inverted, bonnet facing down and boot open, and as the oil slowly seeps away I know with shocking finality that I have killed the couple. But I feel the man's life beat. He is strong but wounded and will never be the same again. I wonder if he will ever drive again.

And as I enter hazy oblivion I watch the stamps flutter down slowly like sycamore seeds in the spring.

L J Silver

Today I shot a man. This is what I do; I kill people for money.

I absently adjust my tortoiseshell glasses on the bridge of my nose, run a hand through grey, receding hair, and wait for the alarm to sound off. Airport security tense up and the Customs Officer beckons me politely to step to one side as he flicks through my passport attentively. Today I am John Silver but I have many names; Juan de la Plata, Jean Argentan; Silvester John. In the cafés of Paris, I am Longues-Jean Silvere.

'Where have you been this weekend, Mr. Silver?' the officer says in a studied, carefree tone, browsing through the liberal collection of European destinations that clog up my passport.

'Sweden, Norway,' I say. *The truth.*

'Business?'

'Vacation,' I answer. *A lie.*

He stares at me with steady, unwavering eyes. He has skill; he knows that long pauses and increased eye contact reap rewards. I know this too; like I know that silence to many more questions, just as too many words uttered, reflect guilt.

'The Northern Lights,' I say.

'Sorry?'

'*Aurora Borealis.* I chased the Lights down in Scotland last year but thought I'd take a closer look in Scandinavia. Stunning.' *Maybe I could be an actor in another life?*

'Why has the alarm activated, Mr. Silver?' he asks after another well-timed pause.

'A grenade fragment.'

Raised eyebrows.

'In my heel.'

'And how did you acquire that?' he says with a thin smile.

'French Foreign Legion in '86,' I say. *Lies doused with truth are often the most believable cover.*

'Thank you, Mr. Silver. Forgive the excessive thoroughness. We are currently on high alert due to an undisclosed event.'

I will disclose it. This morning I shot the Deputy Prime Minister while he was moose hunting in Norway. I am pleased to say it was one shot straight through the heart. I was anxious I would miss. My new glasses just don't feel comfortable with a gun scope. You can't make mistakes in my line of work. Miss a target, word leaks out and you find yourself hanging from a chain in a disused warehouse. No one appreciates the latent threat of an unemployable assassin.

When you read of my handiwork in the press later today, it will speak of an unfortunate accident during a hunting expedition with the Norwegian Foreign Minister. Apparently they were discussing the implications of their current European status. But it was my bullet, my gun. I don't know why he had to die. When I pulled the trigger today I felt empty. The more shots I take the deeper this feeling enters me. The futility of my profession. I have stacked up enough money in this life to make most men envious. I should just walk away. Back to my roots; a well-trained nomad with a gun.

'Life is just a chasing after the wind,' the Abbot used to say. Not his words, he said, King Solomon's. When I was recovering in the Italian Monastery I never read a single word of the Good Book. I just rested while the gunshot wounds healed until I could walk again. Silent monks are good listeners but I had nothing to say. My life has just been a shameful trail of death; until the boy.

I found Slightly hiding, half-starved in the remaining wall of a bombed-out house. He was thin and weak but his eyes were wide and alert; alive. I had always been alone before, walking the length of countries, focussed but without care, notching up experience and assignments like a prisoner counts days to freedom.

On that first day, when I pulled him out of the brickwork and offered him stale bread with hands blackened by the soot of gunpowder, he rarely left my side. The scrappy looking dog came later. Another stray but with the same strong eyes and aggressive instinct for survival. I tried to shake them off – I find closeness uncomfortable – but they surprised me with their stamina and tenacious scrounging abilities. He idolised me; wanted to be like me. Like a sponge he absorbed everything I taught him. *Everything*. Slightly can strip down an AK-47; he can clean and oil it faster than I. I taught him a profession. I learned him to kill. I rescued him, didn't I?

How do you atone for a wasted life?

***

The blonde woman who serves me in the airport coffee house has large eyes the colour of seawater; Mediterranean blue. She has slow hands that operate the equipment clumsily but her pretty, if slightly false smile, is forgiving, as is the Grande Americano which I dose liberally with brown sugar. A post-flight pep up.

My head begins to feel woozy and legs twitchy as I hail a black London cab. The comfort of large rear seats and air conditioning is more than welcome as I enjoy the final syrupy shot of unstirred coffee. It's a slow drive through busy streets and the assorted noises of open-front cafés and the deluge of rush hour traffic penetrates the interior. My device vibrates at an incoming message and I am surprised that a new target has been sent to me so quickly, and unusually, by the same client. I am perplexed; this is rare and crosses the boundary of accepted protocol. When the encrypted file is polished and eventually deposited onto my screen, I am shocked by the image before me. The Mediterranean blue eyes and thin mouth of the target, Elizabeth Fontaine, smile back at me falsely.

The wooziness dissipates like coloured dye in water. I desperately fight to focus and connect the obvious; something big was at play here and I had just got caught right in the middle. My legs are ungainly and stiff when I vacate the cab. Slow poisons do that to you. I thought of calling Slightly, but what would I say? Hey, Slightly, I'm dying?

I shuffle to my allotment, my place of respite, stooped and shivering like one of the drugged vagrants down by the Thames on a cold night. I have a red and white striped deckchair in the hut. It's fraying but comfy and I just want to sit there like I do occasionally on Sunday mornings. I like to watch the goldfinches jumping between seed heads. I never cared much for nature, it was just terrain to be battled against or something moving to be killed and eaten. Age changes you. If you come here at night you can watch moths dive-bombing the amber glow of the street lamps. Just flickering. Did I ever do that or was that what I wanted to do?

As my legs finally give way and my doubling vision morphs into blurry disconnection, I topple onto freshly watered earth amongst rows of neatly planted carrots. The phone rings four times before I recognise the sound and gather my remaining strength to answer it.

'Silver, I'm stuck in a tree, come get me.'

'Slightly?' I say, my voice thick.

'Silver, come get me, the parachute is caught and I've mislaid my knife.'

'Slightly, abandon the assignment.'

'What?'

'Abandon.'

'Your line's breaking up Silver. What do you want me to do?'

'Slightly, abandon de poste. Pour toujours.'

The damp earth I rest in has the scent of a fox.

Slightly

—❧—

Abandon de poste. Pour toujours.

Is that what he said? Silver only reverted to French *parlais* when he was stressed or something was important. It was the first language we used to communicate. I redial several times but he does not pick up the phone. As my parachute sways in the ever-increasing wind I am reminded of the shot I will have to take, and look over at a rooftop garden restaurant that I see lit up in the dusk about a quarter of a mile away. No one will be looking for me here. The shot will be clean and precise, and the target will be dead within the hour. But something doesn't feel right. Silver's words unsettle me. Is that what he said, *abandon de poste?* This assignment is big money. Really big. Silver said I was a better shot. I should take it. Silver said that.

Silver wouldn't be cross that I got caught in a tree because the fact that I can even land on this particular roof shows precision and skill. He would be really angry that I forgot the knife. It is his number one item of kit. You can manage without a water bottle or matches but with a knife you can make shelter, catch food. You can kill a man.

Silver won't answer so I dial the only other number on my phone.

'Doctor Holiday,' a male voice answers politely but with an acidic edge.

'Hi Doc. It's me, Slightly.'

'Uh? . . . How did you obtain my private number?'

'I walk outside the lines, Doc, you know that.'

'Slightly, it's late, I'm at the Albert Hall with my wife, listening to the London Philharmonic. They're about to move into the first notes of the 1812 overture . . . Speak to my secretary, I believe there is a slot available a week Tuesday.'

'I need to speak now, Doc.'

'Slightly . . .'

'I'll wire you five hundred in the morning.'

'It's not the money, I promised my wife . . .'

'I'm sorry. I need to talk and there is no one else. I haven't got anyone else, you know that. Doc?' I wait in the gap, listening to the classical music. I can almost hear his mind reluctantly turning.

'It sounded like Silver told me to abandon my position today.'

'Then do it. You told me you look up to him as a father figure.' I can sense the exasperation in Doc's tone.

'But I'm not sure.'

'Well ask him again.' Doc's coming across terse.

'I can't, he won't answer. I'm worried . . . I'm worried he's gone.'

'Slightly, not everyone's going to leave you,' he says softly, 'it's tragic what has happened in your life but you shape your future. You. Not anyone else.'

'Everyone else I have loved is gone. Even the dog.'

'Animals are loyal but they get distracted.'

A pause. Doc doesn't like dogs.

'In our last session you asked me if I remember anything happy from my past,' I say.

'Yes.'

'Once, when I got sent home from school for stealing, my father whipped me with his belt and sent me to bed without any supper. When everyone was asleep, my mother crept in silently. She wiped my tears with the tattered corners of her dress. She gave me a chunk of stale bread. It was the best meal I ever had.'

Doc is silent and all I hear is flutes and oboes.

'Her dress was orange,' I add.

'That's good, Slightly. Memories will help you. Don't suppress them.' His voice is soft now, like it normally is in his office.

'Thanks, Doc. Enjoy your show.'

I didn't really need a knife; I just wanted to hear the reassurance of Silver's voice. So I double over, study the way the rope has caught in the branches and untangle it using the best method I know how: with intense effort.

This private roof garden is incredible. It's like a jungle up here. You wouldn't believe you are in England, let alone London. But it is nothing compared to the designer rooftop restaurant that my gun scope enlarges. It is green and lush and busy with society's pretty people, arriving to drink champagne and eat line-caught Alaskan Salmon, cooked in complicated sauces by celebrity chefs. Exotic ingredients imported from Europe and the Far East.

I am not interested in pretty people. I am interested in the Prime Minister. My gun sight is pointed at his head as if I were seated next to him, talking to his inner circle about asylum seekers and the constant influx of refugees. I know nothing of politics, but I do know death and hunger and desperation. I know what a man will do for food. I know the length a woman will go to save her child. I know.

Abandon de poste?

The shot is clear and easy. Silver and I could retire on the money. Maybe even buy a small island in the Caribbean. My finger rests on the curve of the trigger. We could repair a small boat and spend days fishing the Mediterranean or drive old cars in the dusty roads of South America. We could stop running.

Silver: Abandon de poste. Pour toujours. Today?

Silver's voice I hear clearly, so with a silent goodbye to the Prime Minister I disassemble the rifle and try and figure out how I will leave this building unnoticed.

I think of the curly-haired dog that sat with me in the darkness and briefly wonder whether he still smells of seaweed.

Doc Holiday

Music: Tchaikovsky's 1812 Overture.

Memories can't be trusted. They are fragmented, broken. The truth coloured in. We make a nice story of the fragments we find.

I ponder the painted image of Slightly's mother. Did she ever wear an orange dress or bring him bread in the quiet hours of the night? Did she wipe his tears? Or is that what he wanted to remember – an isolated moment of love in a life of suffering? It's like I said to the policeman, early Saturday morning when he took my statement with stubby pencil held between nail-bitten fingers:

'I can tell you what I think I saw, Officer.'

'What you think you saw?' he replies.

'Yes. The brain. It connects fragments of memory, adds presumption from learned experience and produces its own narrative.'

'What?'

'I can tell you the best version of the truth I know.'

He looks at me with distaste and poised pen.

'What do you *think* you saw, Doctor Holiday?'

'Well, I was jogging through the southern gate of the park, underneath the lion, probably around 6:45. My laps of the park are becoming a lot faster. Yes, definitely 6:45. That's when I heard the car.'

'Were you running into the park, or out and along Barnard Avenue?'

'Out and along. I heard the car tyres, so it must have been travelling fast. It's supposed to be 20mph around here. The engine was noisy too.'

'When you say *the car*, do you mean that one over there?' He pointed at the crumpled mess of a black VW Golf flipped on its bonnet.

'Yes.'

'And that was the only car?'

'Er . . . I think so.'

'And did you see the driver?'

'Yes, I remember him because he looked directly at me. Then straight at the couple before he drove into them.'

'What? You think he drove directly at them?' he says with a frown.

'Well, I'm not saying that . . . but he did have determined eyes.'

'Determined eyes?'

'Well, dark eyes. Brown, yes definitely brown. They seemed brown when he crawled from the car.'

'You saw him crawl from the car?'

'Yes. I would have helped him but . . . I couldn't stop looking at the bodies, there was so much blood.'

I put a hand over my mouth but I still managed to be sick, spraying the policeman's scuffed shoes. 'Sorry,' I say timidly. I'm sure he understood. It's not an everyday occurrence; the sight of limbs twisted in the wrong direction.

'Was the man hurt? That car has taken quite a battering,' he says after a long silence while gazing at his shoes.

'He was holding his head,' I say.

'What was he like? What was he wearing?'

'Youngish; maybe 30. Brown hair, dark eyes.'

'I thought you said brown eyes?'

'Yes, dark brown.'

'Clothes?'

'White shirt. Dark denim. Brown shoes. He escaped down Barnaby Avenue.'

'Were there any other witnesses?'

'No. But I thought I saw a small dog.' I chuckle half-heartedly at the obscure image.

'There's nothing funny in this Doctor Holiday. Two people have died.' As the officer walks off I shout to him, 'What are all those coloured squares floating around everywhere?'

'Postage stamps,' he replies.

That was last Saturday. Now when I look back all I can see is the dead bodies of two young lovers, twisted in a sickening embrace. And on the edge of my vision, the curly-haired dog running next to a skipping girl, beneath a lion statue.

Tchaikovsky pulls me back to the present; the harmonious notes a tonic to the stresses of life. I close my eyes and attempt to isolate each instrument in my mind. Oboes, cornets, trombones; the subtle pick-me-up of the flute. I am concentrating, not thinking; trying not to ruin the musical moment I am caught up in.

But I can't concentrate. Too much has happened recently and I am trying to piece it all together and wrestle with the overriding feeling that I should not be sitting contentedly while a family has been destroyed by the death of that young couple. And how I can sit here knowing the tickets for tonight's show were a thousand pounds apiece and I am now precisely £451,350 in debt!

Yes, over £450K! I may live in the correct post code and have the most prestigious designer craft my suit, but last week I had nothing and was ready to go into administration. Nothing; nada, ixnay! It's all very well having a successful practise but if you can't control your wife's liberal use of plastic you will never have enough. Never!

At wits' end I went to the local church and visited the Priest. He physically balked at the size of the debt when I spilled all, but had no magic solution. However, he did pray for me and said he would again the next day, and told me to come back when God answers. I looked him in the eye; he was serious. The next day he called me early and said he dreamt of me posting an envelope. I was smiling, he said. I asked why. Because of what was in the envelope, he said. It was your confession to God; you had written out everything you had done wrong in this life. You were pleased to get it off your chest; pleased to dispose of it.

I thought the Priest was a nutcase, but when he hung up I began to think on my mistakes; dwell on the things that kept me awake at night.

That was the day before the crash. When I jogged home after the incident I felt too jaded to face a list of clients with unending, unsolvable problems. I now had too many of my own.

After the crash I decided to take a day off and changed from my sweaty track suit into some sports slacks. It was then that the stamps fell out; they were stuck in my hood. Five of them. Different years; different countries.

When I arrived at the café, the usual crowd of successful semi-retired caffeine junkies sat at haphazard tables. Together yet apart; enjoying each other's company but comfortable in their own space. I nodded to Figgis, who was diligently working on the *Guardian* crossword and walked over to Blumenfeld, who was propped up in the corner reading the *Financial Times*, drinking a double expresso.

'Having a good day, Holiday?' he says.

'I've had better,' I say in understatement, trying to shake off a sudden flashback to broken bones. There is a long, uncomfortable silence which Blumenfeld never fills, so I place the five stamps on the table. That gets his attention; Blumenfeld collects stamps with a strange fervour that I can only liken to that of a fanatical football fan.

'Where did you get this?' he asks with serious eyes, pointing to the end stamp that is messy and pink and non-descript.

'What?'

'Where did you get it?'

'It was in my track suit hood after my run this morning.'

He looks around the café to see if anyone is looking.

'Doc, that is the *1 Cent Magenta!*' he says to me in hushed excitement.

'What?'

'The *1 Cent Magenta.* It's one of the rarest stamps in the world.'

'Is it valuable?' I say, not sharing his excitement or apparent knowledge.

'Valuable! It's worth a fortune!'

By the end of our short coffee together, the stamp has been picked up with tweezers, placed in an airtight container and was on its way to auction with Blumenfeld, its happy courier.

When the last notes of the *1812* give way to applause my phone rings again and despite the withering look I receive from my wife, I answer, thinking it must be Slightly.

'Holiday, it's me,' says a husky excitable voice.

'Blumenfeld?'

'Yes Doc. Do you want the good news or the bad news?'

'I haven't got time ...'

'There is no bad news, Doc, your stamp just sold for £451,350! How about that!'

'How much?' I say, incredulously.

'£451,350! You're rich Doc!'

But I don't think of the money; I think of the letter I need to post.

SUDDEN DEATH OF FRANK CAPLIN SPARKS ENQUIRY

The sudden death of Frank Caplin prior to an independent televised debate has many in our nation mourning. Although it is clear that he had many fights with cancer, there were no obvious signs of remission and a few of his outspoken supporters have openly suggested foul play. Frank was a breath of fresh air to a tired nation. Fed up with corrupt politicians, he openly challenged those he dubbed as 'career politicians', who worked for money rather than the people. Brought out of retirement by a Labour Party who could not find anyone remotely media friendly, Frank said that he just wanted to help his country through this difficult time. Softly spoken but with an acidic edge, political commentators believe Frank clearly had no agenda other than to speak the truth to a nation that is on the decline thanks to what he describes as 'decades of mismanagement and corruption'. The televised debate, centring on the current immigration issues and the troubled exit from Europe, was set to take place with the Deputy Prime Minister and young Conservative hopeful, Francis Glib, who is rumoured to be backed financially by media tycoon Sir Anthony Develaire. The death of the Deputy Prime Minister in Norway this week has seen the nation on high alert, although authorities have clearly stated that this was an accident due to misfire of a hunting rifle. While the nation will grieve doubly this week, Glib has offered to speak live on television and unite the parties in both mourning and a way forward with Europe and the immigration debate. Develaire refused to comment, indicating as always that he has no political bias and was just interested in reporting the news.

Samantha (Just)

—⁀ೞ⁀—

I must be clean! The lingering smell of vomit detaches me from the present. Dazed, I walk into my building, ignoring the pleasant greetings from the new girl on reception. Usually I would assess her for objects to steal but I must get clean. *I must get clean.* When I reach my office, I dump the bike messenger's bag and run into the shower fully clothed. As the water becomes hotter I frantically rip off my clothes and leave the sodden pile to clog up the drain, forming a gradually increasing pool beneath my feet.

In the shower I see:

> Steam rising (like smoke from a fire)
> Uncountable droplets of water
> Long fingers and dirty, broken fingernails
> Purple scented soap hanging from knotted string
> A reflection of the gold cross around my neck
> and a distressed face mirrored back at me.

Much later, when the fear has subsided and continuous scrubbing has cleansed me of the rancid smell of blood and vomit, and replaced it with a perfumed scent and the natural aroma of hot skin, I ponder on the man in the hat. Nobody kills for a camera – they just steal it, don't they?

I feel vulnerable without clothes so I put my coat on; it is grey with a herringbone weave. I stole it from Maggie in Accounts last October; she had too many coats anyway. I prefer her in the rain jacket and told her so when she was searching for it. It is a winter coat, so I find the pale blue hat and scarf and sit at my desk thinking of the 'snow day' when I watched Amelia in the park with Stephen.

Amelia.

When I feel anxious I like to view and categorise my collections. Firstly the leaves stuck in the brown scrapbook. Some are dry and brittle now, so I turn the pages carefully not wanting to break them and spoil the memories of the little girl in wellies who ran through them laughing.

I break out Notebook number 7; it's nearly new so the pages are crisp and white. I smell them because who doesn't like the smell of a new book. The last conversations written in there are between Brandon in Sales and the new girl. The words are pointless and sickly; thankfully he was unaware that he is a good distraction as I rooted through her Jimmy Choo bag to pilfer red lipstick.

My favourite conversations are between me and my silent friend whilst we drink breakfast tea in the café over the road from the church. I remember each conversation exactly, word for word. They are like a clear photograph, framed in my mind. The precious words I write carefully with a black ink pen. It upsets me if I smudge them, which can happen even with the best fountain pen, but a Biro is not important enough to record the words we share. The words must be perfect; not forgotten. I fill in the blanks, imagining what he would reply, if he could speak, imagining what he would say as I spill every dark detail out. He would give good advice, I know it. It is enough that he listens. He is my only friend. Would he mind that I stole his cross? This bothers me. But I need it. I touch it when I am sleeping. It comforts me in the night when the shadows of the past haunt me.

Would my friend miss me today? Would he drink tea without me? If only I hadn't followed the bike messenger. The thought of him makes me shudder with all that blood running freely, pooling on the lift floor. And the long barrelled gun held by the tall man in the wide-brimmed hat.

The thought of his death makes me anxious so I start to look through my photos. Firstly a collection of flower photographs taken by Alice, the bike messenger's girlfriend. I stole them some months back when I sat next to her on the train. I was disappointed that the bike messenger didn't leave with her that day, a sunny trip to Southend. But I liked the way he kissed her gently with open eyes when they parted. There were only thirty photos in her bag that day. Beautiful characterisations of honeybees on yellow and white flowers. Oh, and one of a curly haired dog with a stone in his mouth. I liked them so much that I didn't steal anything else. I just spent the day on the pier eating ice cream and watching seagulls scavenge for bread.

The photographs remind me that I have the bike messenger's memory card and I slot it into the laptop, only to be disappointed. No photos, just a video file, which I double click to play and maximise the screen because the image is dark, and turn the volume right up because it is silent. Nothing. Just an orange fox walking casually across an empty car park. It looks at the camera then jumps on the bonnet of an old blue car.

I hear the handle of the door turning and could kick myself for not locking it in my rush to get clean. And there before me stands my friend, with a worried look on his face.

'How did you find me?' I say. He found me, I think happily.

He smiles. Then he frowns and is looking at the screen, not me. The video was still running and now the vacant car park is busy. This is what I see:

Two men
The man in the wide-brimmed hat
A man in black (he scares me and I want to turn it off)
A fox's eyes
The sound of quiet breathing
A shiny black car
A hushed singsong voice.

The conversation between the men goes like this. I remember the words but I don't want to put them in my book.

'The Deputy PM is expendable. He must *remain* in Norway. Don't mess up.'

'I have sent an asset. His death will look like an accident, Mr. Develaire.'

'Make sure it is professional. You are paid good money for this. I don't want further questions, not like Caplin's death. We can only *buy* so many policemen.'

I feel afraid, even though my silent friend stands next to me. Fear is irrational; I know this. But it pervades my peace until all rationality is dissolved. I worry about my most precious gift. I must see her. I must see Amelia!

Grey (Inspector)

—ɞ ɠ—

Browning automatic.

I could feel the gun resting heavily in the creased fabric of my cheap suit. Evidence, stolen from the Station. I'm not sure why I took it but I started breaking the rules the day after she disappeared. That first day it was speeding; 103mph on an A road, and I'd been drinking. I flashed my badge and walked away lazily. Finally some merit to rank.

The sad thing about breaking rules is that once you've broken one it becomes a habit. Your life slowly unravels and the criminals and lowlifes, like that idiot Layton, begin to seem like allies. Was Henderson a wasted opportunity? My world is now grey; the clarity and definition of black and white now dissolved, each colour merged and indiscernible from the other.

When the Audi choked on the last dregs of diesel for the third time in a month, I drifted into the hard shoulder and alighted from the vehicle, only to be hit by a wall of heat and a slight aroma of blackberries hanging from thorn-laden tentacles, threatening to ensnare my feet. I absently held one between two fingers, tasted its sticky sweetness and watched the reddy-black juices stain my skin. Like blood, it's difficult to remove once spilt.

I didn't care for the car or the officer who would reluctantly pick it up. For a change I just wanted to go home; sleepless nights and alcohol take their toll.

The easiest route home was up and over the gantry, and across a series of fields. If I walked in a straight line I figured it would take me maybe 25 minutes, 30 tops if I had to skirt around the brown bull in the field behind *The Cricketers*.

So I climb the ringed ladder; it is locked with a shiny padlock but there is clearly enough room for entry. I run along this makeshift bridge, taking care not to trip on the thick electrical wires. From the top I look down on the rushing Friday traffic. Why is everyone in this damned country so ridiculously busy? It doesn't stop unless you are dead, like Henderson or Caplin. Frank Caplin, now that is something that doesn't add up. *'Died of a long-term illness'* – that line stinks and sounds as fake as the second hand of the Breitling that rests on my wrist. *Evidence.* Caplin spent months aggressively challenging the integrity of the media and politicians close to the Prime Minister, now he is dead. When you have watched crime unfold as long as I have, the patterns leave a trace imprinted like a lightbulb stared at too long.

It bothered me releasing Layton, but I couldn't quite place why. I just knew that this odd character with a sketchy, mislaid past would surface again. Whether his destiny was behind bars or floating face down in the Thames I cannot predict, but I felt certain we would meet again. The blonde girl on the horse was another matter. A ghost! How can you kill a man with a horse and leave no reliable digital trace? It's supposed to be the twenty-first century!

The long grasses I drop into from the loosely enclosed ladder scratch at my hand with sharp seed heads and I'm already covered in dust and pollen when I arrive at the gate.

The hum of the motorway begins to fade and the dry smell of fumes is gradually replaced with the distant scent of wild garlic, assorted grasses and flowers. Before me cabbage whites flutter between patches of nettles and a sea of long-stemmed buttercups carpet the way ahead, their yellow petals moving gently as I brush past and soak in the idyllic. I should have been a garden designer instead of a policeman, creating wild flower meadows for rich widows rather than being slowly polluted by this nation's scum.

The bull is young and patrols the field behind *The Cricketers* like a cadet on training. I don't trust it not to fire so I jump the fence and wet my feet in the stream, and follow the remnants of Red House Lane until I reach the inn; across from it is my cottage.

Butterfly Cottage always surprises me with its postcard simplicity; hollyhocks and foxgloves peak over a dry stone wall; an ancient rose rambles across a crafted pergola. Rustic country elegance. It was what first caught my eye when we first saw the property one sunny day in June.

But now as I go through the gate I'm wary, because even from here I can tell the door's been forced. I feel fear creep in and instinctively reach for the gun in my pocket. An unloaded gun is placeboic security. I changed the locks the day she disappeared. Subconscious fear is the hardest to erase. I didn't want her back in. I didn't.

When I nudge the door open with the muzzle I unconsciously reach for the place where my ribs were broken. The scars are in my mind. Doused with fear I look back at the inn and long to cross over and pour alcohol onto my wound; I long to let it soak in and soften the ache of it. Where it once took two, now it takes three or four jars of amber ale. A liquid that now tastes bitter and has no lasting effect.

There is no fear in love, the counsellor said. Fear opposes love.

I check each room with caution, then tenacity as the hefty assurance of the gun begins to induce false confidence. Is not part of a gun the bluff of its use? Bullets are for killers. Those who can cross the line.

Through the wooden kitchen door I step cautiously onto the gravel path. When I turn the handle to the shed door the memories flood in with a sharp intake of breath. It is here on top of the relative comfort of a bag of compost I learnt that a man can eventually sleep; sketchy, broken sleep, crouched in a corner, wrapped in hessian sacks smelling of old seed potatoes. I pissed in a cracked pint glass that night; and the night after.

The garden is neat with well-kept green grass and beautifully flowered borders; carefully chosen mixes that attract bees and butterflies. Moving colours. I recall there was a green woodpecker once, tapping on the silver birch. *Betula pendula.* You can't see the entire garden from the house so when I reach the bird bath, hidden beneath the dappled shade of red maple leaves, the summer house eventually strays into view. It's beautiful in white-washed wood, guarded by bright green topiary pots. I can't remember the last time I felt relaxed enough to read a book in there. Zusak, Hinton, Hemingway; the memoirs of dead war correspondents. Pages to escape in.

The doors are open and to my surprise a bottle of Barbaresco '67 sits still and breathing next to a glass. I can smell the aroma; dried roses. Whoever chose this bottle knows me; I haven't drunk this wine since a sunny afternoon underneath the Eiffel Tower in 2008. It's not cheap; it's not easy to find.

I pick up the glass and look through the complexity of colour and think of the blackberries by the motorway, and let the taste of it take me back to France. Carefree; another life. And the fear is gone because she did not know this wine or its French origin in my life. I carried it in my backpack from Dieppe. And as I think of the implications of this gesture or message I notice a strip of paper with hand-written numbers underneath the bottle. Coordinates.

When I tap them into my phone and walk out my front door and down Red House Lane, I instinctively know the GPS will lead me to the disused phone box that is half-buried in an overgrown privet hedge.

The red paint is peeling from the phone box and the dirty glass is cracked and green with mould. I look up and down the road with practised caution, but only my imagination sees things beyond the emptiness. I search with practised skill; it takes me ten minutes to find it. A metal geocache ingeniously concealed within a carefully cut away receiver. Inside the cache, rolling alongside a fox brooch and an eyepatch, are six 9mm bullets.

As I load the empty gun I sense that today I would cross a line. I don't believe in coincidence.

Kerith Ravine (The Brook)

—⁓⁓—

Then the word of the LORD came to Elijah: 'Leave here, turn east-ward and hide in the Kerith Ravine, east of the Jordan. You will drink from the brook ...' **1 Kings 17: 2–4**

***

Samantha is crying and I don't know what to do. She sits amongst the photos, looking, searching. I feel her anxiety – it penetrates my skin. What is it? What is wrong, I want to say, but no words come out.

'I can't find her! I can't find her!' she says with urgency.

Who?

She is rocking and sobbing and holding the cross around her neck and I can't comfort her.

'I gave away my baby. I gave away my baby,' she repeats over and over.

What?

'I gave away my baby!' she screams and I duck as a glass flies through the air, shattering on the wall above my head. I have never seen her like this. It scares me. And the shattered fragments lie underfoot with hundreds upon hundreds of glossy photos, and now her frantic hands are bleeding from a myriad of cuts. Blood drips on snapshots of a pretty girl with bunches and gapped teeth.

Stop! I want to shout, but there is no sound so my arms stretch out to hold her. I pull her close, surprised by her lightness, disarmed by her warmth. Then she sees it; a black and white square; the hazy beginnings of life; a baby's foetus.

'My baby,' she says and looks at me with tear-streaked face, 'Something is wrong, I feel it.' And she gets up and runs and I try and follow her, but she is quick like a greyhound chasing a hare. Her red sneakers barely touch carpet as I follow corridor upon corridor and step after step until we reach the roof-top after bursting into light and air through a fire exit. I wonder where she is going because she hasn't slowed up and I wish she would stop because it's dangerous up high with loose gritty shingle and no railings. And she astounds me, as with either complete confidence or a careless disregard for life, she jumps and flies through the air and lands on the adjacent building. She turns, looks at me once, and is gone.

And I stand on the edge, nauseous because heights fill me with fear. I'm really angry with myself and my weakness. Now I found her, I had no intention of letting her go. But she is gone, slipped away like a pickpocket in a crowded market.

I slowly walk back to her room, trying to navigate the confusion of conflicting thoughts. I want to find her, but where would I look? I feel a responsibility to hand in the memory card – but how could I explain it to the police? I have no voice and my shirt is covered with blood from Samantha's cut fingers! I look like I've been dragged through the dirtied edge of a crime scene. I can't even remember my name!

I sit on the floor just like Sam did earlier and gradually sift through photographs of the beautiful girl who has the same round face as her mother; the same eyes. A little girl with rosy cheeks, red wellies and a blue raincoat. It surprises me but I never regarded Sam as beautiful before, I never thought about it. But the thought of her missing tugs at me painfully inside. Her absence hurts me. Deeply. How has this woman got so inside of me?

Two more albums, clothed in taupe suede, are stacked on the desk like paperwork files in an office. They are crammed with photos. The first was filled with shots of high-ceilinged rooms and a pretty square courtyard garden; a Victorian house. The photos are portrait and set neat and exact; four per page. Samantha is precise, particular. Each room has three pages of photos devoted to its contents. The kitchen: photos of eggs in a basket, a mug with a red heart and the words 'I love you', white carnations in a smoky blue vase. And a square bedroom: a metal frame bed, purple alliums embroidered on a crisp white duvet, teddies lined in a row. Each one photographed separately – named with an artistic flourish in hand-written pencil: Chips, Fleur, Foxley . . .

When I open the second album, a wave of emotion catches me

thick and sudden in the back of my throat. And I weep uncontrollably at a man and woman kissing by a red door. As I lay there amongst the photos and blood and glass, the tears wouldn't stop and I didn't know why. I feel so angry because I don't know what to do. I don't know what to do. I don't know!

I cry myself to sleep.

In my dreams scriptures like memories reappear randomly like shooting stars on a cold winter's night. I grab at them before they disappear into the cobwebbed recesses and disconnected compartments in my mind.

His word runs swiftly.
I will not forget you, I have engraved you on the palms of my hands.
His way is in the whirlwind and the storm . . . His way.

In this subconscious state, memories of my past flood back in and I embrace them warmly. Large, calloused hands reach out and haul me up to the dizzy heights of broad shoulders. My soft hair gets tusselled in the wind. This giant is my father. A man of few words; patient, kind.

It's a hot day and the bus is stifling as we make our way home from school. The bus halts on a roundabout, the queue of cars ahead long and never ending. Heat ripples from tarmac.

'What's happened, Dad?'

'Looks like an accident. Come on, let's go.'

'It's too far to walk,' I moan.

'I'll carry you.'

And he nods to the bus driver who opens the doors, and we are gone. That day, while passengers sat frustrated as minutes turned into hours, Dad and I played in the park and ate chocolate ice cream. We visited grandparents and spoke to strangers. Dad made good decisions.

In my mind's eye, Dad lifts me down and when I reach the floor I'm walking through grass on the edge of a wood, and now I am tall like my father. He is greying now and there is tiredness in his eyes, but he is strong inside; his faith sustains him. I know this because his words speak it out.

It is a long and pleasant walk through grassy terrain and we share long silences and technical discussions on Kepler's Laws of Planetary Motion, before reaching a copse of trees where my father shows some caution.

'Blackwood said that Churchill was here one time during the war. But he didn't say why.'

I start to move closer when I spy the concrete edges of a heavily camouflaged bunker, but Dad's hand lay heavy on my shoulder.

'It could still be rigged with explosives. The Fox Club were a little untidy back then.'

'I thought history was supposed to be climbed on and touched?'

'Not this time, Son.'

'Who was the greatest Prime Minister of Britain Dad?' I say with a smile, as we walk back, already knowing his answer.

'Winston Churchill.'

A pause.

'Churchill was a great man. He knew his calling.'

You may not believe me but I was awoken by a Still Small Voice. A whisper.

Leave here.

So I leave the building with no idea of where to go or what to do. No direction. Until I hear the distinctive noise of a Merlin engine overhead. Waves of nostalgia hit me and I hear the words of my father, 'Spitfires heading east. Peace through conflict.' I look up and gaze at the dark, elliptical wings above me, and my heart leaps with the certainty of knowing.

Turn eastward.

I follow the lone Spitfire until it is a minute dot between an isolated expanse of clouds. When it is gone, I follow the reassuring noise of its engine, and when that has disappeared I confidently pursue the memory of sound and continue walking east. I am unaware of people walking beside me or the busyness of traffic. I just look up at the clouds, expectant. I sense the iconic plane has vanished but the direction is set.

When the sun rises for a second time I am parched and half delirious as I drop to my knees in a clearing in a wood. The bracken beneath me crunches with dryness and ants scurry forward to discover the intrusion. There is a silence except the confusion and noise in my head, which returns to eat away at me. Now I am thirsty and broken with exhaustion. I don't know what to do. Did God really call me out here? Why would he?

I smell the water but cannot see it. Its unspoken freshness calls to me and on hands and knees I crawl past the clearing and drop into the dry banks of a brook to drink from the tiny silver thread that remains. My thirst is quenched and my aching need for sleep overrides the growling of my stomach. The brown dust by the brook sticks to my lips as I rest in the tranquillity of this basin, and I imagine a crisp, white duvet with purple alliums lined in a row.

I sleep deeply only to awake once in the night as an owl hoots nearby. And with one eye open I see the brightness of the moon between the darkened outline of leaves. My limbs ache and compete with the pangs of hunger that gnaw away at me. When was the last time I had eaten? I sleep and then sleep some more.

I am woken by penetrating sunlight high in the sky, and a small, curly haired dog sniffing my feet in an unthreatening manner. He rolls around on his back in the dust. He smells of seaweed. My eyes shut and he is gone. When he returns, the corner of a red checked picnic rug is gripped tightly between his off-white teeth. Caught in the corner is a small plastic box. Half-eaten ham sandwiches laced with mustard and a wedge of cheese lie within a bed of broken crisps and green grapes, which the dog tries desperately to snaffle. I rescue the sandwiches and cheese and let my unusual companion crunch his way through the remains of broken crisps.

I *hide in the brook,* alone, apart from the flea-bitten company of the fortuitous dog. I watch the stars appear gradually and the sun rise and set many times until the brook dries up and the dog vanishes into the hidden pockets of the night.

Early morning I hear the peeling of a bell. I leave the relative comfort of the brook and cautiously walk along a little-used trail bordered by high grasses and overhanging trees. I startle a deer in the field adjacent and listen to the competing melody of dual skylarks hovering above. The bell is solemn and constant and I am drawn to the sound and its origin: a small, brick church – a solitary building in a field on the crest of a hill. The churchyard is populated with huddles of black-suited mourners who loiter amongst ancient off-kilter gravestones. They stare at my blood and dirt-encrusted shirt with curiosity as I intrude on their grief like a gunslinger in a bar full of strangers.

The quiet chatter of mourners ceases, as does the ringing of the bell, and all eyes look in my direction, except for the dog who is curled up sleeping in the shade of a hawthorn tree. And through the gathering silence I hear the muffled sound of a phone ringing and walk towards the people who are moving away from a coffin finished in light oak and polished brass.

The coffin opens easily, as I knew it would, and I draw a deep intake of breath and reach inside the brown striped jacket of the unfortunate corpse, and silence the vibrating phone with a single touch. Then, holding it to my ear, I utter broken, hesitant words in the hoarse whisper that is the tattered remains of my voice:

'Sam, I know where your daughter is.'

Pink Striped Musette Bag

—ച ഛ—

My owner lies still and the pink-haired thief who stole me runs with a fear that is contagious. When she finally hangs me up my contents are so jumbled that the cyclist's gel bar has split open. The sticky sweetness has leaked onto the unposted envelope, smudging curly handwritten letters. It's a shame because I feel the letters have been inked thoughtfully, almost as if they had known they would be the last words he would write. *Alice*: underline, space, kiss, space, underline.

If you would open this envelope, this is what he said:

Dear Alice,

It occurred to me that I am a journalist and I've rarely written a single word to you.

I love you.

I don't know why it has been so hard to say these words because it is what I felt when we first spoke under the railway bridge. When I gazed at you I thought you had been crying, but it was the rain on your face. I watched the droplets roll down your cheeks and rest on your lips. That was the moment I knew I wanted to kiss you. I love kissing you, Alice. The way your lips seek mine as if that was all they have ever tasted. What was it that poet said? 'Your breath is my breath.' I know this is true because I feel it deep inside, when I taste you and breathe you in.

You are such a talented photographer. I have probably never said this enough, not out loud anyway. The way you capture the colours in a rainbow or the intricacy of a flower's petal amazes me. Your gift astounds me. A lens in your hands turns ugly people beautiful. Your art has shown me there is something unique in everyone, shown me everything is wonderfully made. Why didn't I ever tell you this?

I loved the pictures of us walking through the fields of corn that hot day in July. Full gold stalks capped by blue skies. And the snapshots of Deputy scampering ahead. How does that dog always find its way home? He's so unusual. We must try and find his real owner; surely someone must be missing him.

When I picture you in my mind, I see you in the white dress with the pink shell necklace resting against your olive skin. I loved the way your eyes looked at me when I gave it to you. I still remember the first touch of your hand. I read somewhere that a longing fulfilled is a tree of life. It's true.

Alice, when I started writing I often wondered whether my words would influence people, inform them, change their perception or opinion. Now I wonder whether there are some stories that should be buried, kept secret, for the greater good. I believe the origins of the Fox Club is one such story. I know everything about them. I could reveal all and expose all things that have been undertaken outside written law. I wrote it all down; perfect words. It would have made the front page of every tabloid and shocked the nation. But I burnt it. I watched the flames destroy the most well-researched, precisely written piece that has ever flowed from my pen. And why? My conscience wouldn't let me publish it. There are some things that should be left unsaid, some stories best untold. National security is not a game.

Last week I was hired by Elisabeth Fontaine! I know who she really is, Alice. The laughable irony is that I, Alex Monroe, now work for the Fox Club! Life has a strange way of completing circles.

Alice, please burn this letter after reading. I fear I have placed us both in danger. Every digital device is being monitored. Every call or text or email. I can't return to the flat. Not yet.

There's some evidence I need you to burn, too. I stumbled across my first lead to the Fox Club when I was compiling Hathaway's obituary. It's hidden behind the Robert Capa photograph in the living room, the one with the young SS officer being searched by military police. Normandy '44. That photograph is worth thousands but the evidence behind is priceless.

I am sorry for all the mistakes I have made. All the words I never said.

I love you.

AM
xxxx

Felis Catus (2)

Not every scent trail should be followed, but when Matka disappeared hunger eventually bested me.

I chased the scruffy rat down a long, ceramic pipe that reeked of fish heads loosely disguised with soap. The bubbles shot up my nose. I sneezed repeatedly and sensed the time for pursuit was over, but kept moving forward anyway. Sometimes you just run without direction, without thinking, and end up somewhere you don't want to be: a dead end, a wrong turn, a dark alley.

The alley I resurfaced in wasn't dark, the sun was still out, which surprised me. The pipe was disorientating and I had lost track of time. The sun was reflecting off cobbled paving and bright leaves from newly planted trees. I watched leaf shadows flutter playfully on white-washed brickwork. Nowhere to be seen, the rat had evaporated into thin air. Rats, I wouldn't choose to eat them but sometimes you take what you can get. The rats are so large in this part of Town that a small cat can easily be caught off guard. Not a cat like me, of course – I have pace and menace. The rats are everywhere. They outnumber us, I tell you, and they are not fussy – **they** eat anything. *Anything.*

Feeling sleepy, I scampered up the white wall and slipped through an open window, landing amongst potted herbs and a collection of seashells, before stepping into a shiny silver sink. The ticking of a clock greeted me as did the lingering smell of burnt toast and peanut butter. I cautiously moved from shiny floor to carpet, brushing my tail against a sofa the colour of milk, and gazed up at brightly coloured pictures of smiling people playing on sand. There was a curly haired dog in the water. It had a stone in its mouth. Dogs have no sense. My eyes hopped from one picture to the next; white flowers, petals falling and a honey bee, silently buzzing in mid-flight. I gazed at the colours, magnetised, because they seemed so real and perfect but were flat and uniform and framed. Memories contained. One picture sat alone and distant on the far wall. The faces in this picture did not smile. They were not in colour; the figure in black and white wore a thick trench coat; his eyes were mean. My eyes were drawn to it and remained there for some time; I sensed something important had been captured in this moment and briefly wished that I was human enough to understand your many faces.

I can sleep anywhere, and the stack of cushions I jumped upon must have been arranged just for me. They sank in to just the right depth and the fabric was softer than my fur. I snuggled into it and I drifted into a peaceful slumber.

My hearing is exceptional, so the noise that woke me was slight. I half expected to see a rat sneaking across the carpet but was surprised to discover the man with *nothing in his eyes* enter the room. His strides are long; at the wall he removes the black and white picture and smashes it on the table. I jump. Amongst shattered glass and wood splinters he pulled out sheets of paper.

'*Fox Club Protocol!*' I hear him whisper into the room. And I look up because I think he is talking to me. But he isn't, and that's when he sees me. I know this because he points a long barrel in my direction. My green eyes stare back into those empty depths of nothingness and the fur on my neck and tail begins to rise, an instinctive response to danger. I see death in front of me but I am ready to fight because I have nine lives and there are still three left.

And then the door opens and a girl enters whistling a happy song, and is shocked into silence when she sees the man and looks at the broken picture.

She screams and now he points the long barrel at her. I fear that he will hurt her like he did poor Matka, so I jump at him with claws sharp and teeth biting. And I spit and snarl and rake the side of his face. The girl runs and a loud noise booms and I see a flash of fire, and in an instant there is a pain in my foot as I drop to the floor. The people disappear but I don't really notice – the pain is too great. It is worse than when that broken roof tile fell on my tail last moon.

My foot is leaking as I limp down the stairs and through the open doorway. The metallic taste sits on my tongue as I lick my paw. This wound confuses my senses so I do not smell the rats in the shadows of the drain, but I see four sets of eyes. They follow me. My paw still leaks as I stagger along the grassy bank of the canal, pursued by dark shapes that smell the scent of weakness. With blurred vision I choose to fall into the murky water to outwit the rats descending upon me. The cold water revives me and my vision steadies as my body floats downstream. I desperately, urgently, completely want to keep a hold of this life. I let out a loud, gurgling miaow, trying to keep my head above water. The boys in blazers walking the bank, kicking dust and swinging satchels above their heads, see me; they point and laugh as I struggle in the water. My foot pulsates.

I save my last loudest miaow for the smartly dressed woman who talks into her hand quickly. She pretends not to see me but I catch her eye before I finally sink beneath the surface. The canal water is dirty with greens and browns and unidentifiable floating objects that hit my body as I begin to black out. And my last thought is of my mother and the kittens that fed alongside me. I wish I had known their names. Where are they now?

The old man who fished me out the canal smelled of trash and stale sweat. He wore an overly large raincoat and glasses; the fur on his face was long and white and scraggy like that ugly house cat that stares from the penthouse down on First.

I black out.

When I awake I smell the sooty heat of a fire. I am stretched out on a wooden table with my paw being sewn up with needle and thread. I howl weakly at the pain – it is sharp and throbbing and when I close my eyes I see rats gnawing at it repeatedly. But it's all in my head.

'It's alright, kitty,' the man says to me, and I fall asleep and dream of fish eyes looking up at me from murky water.

When I awake again I open one eye cautiously and see a young man remove his glasses and the fur from his face, and put them in the drawer under the table. He sits in a worn chair by the fire and writes on small paper sheets with a curly script. He writes until his pen runs out of ink, then he picks up a book and begins reading; it is black with silver writing on the spine.

Much later, when I became strong enough to run on three paws, I returned and found Matka reading in bed by the light of a candle. I snuggled beside her and fell asleep, pleased at last to be home. But some days, when the wind blows cold and long, I reappear on Doctor Edison's table, then sleep by the warmth of his fire, next to empty bottles of ink.

Figgis (The Watchman)

—⁓—

Hackney is a grand place for raising chickens.

I was so absorbed by the exceptionally well-written article on inner city allotments and the success of local residents with root vegetables, that I almost overlooked the absurd sentence.

There in print on page seven of today's *Guardian*, as a precursor to the discussion on the copious and unusual varieties and colours of carrots, were the words: Hackney is a grand place for raising chickens. Complete nonsense, I thought initially. Then my brain slowly caught up with me and I lower the paper cautiously and casually glance around the busy café with practised eyes. Nothing unusual; Alvaro the Puerto Rican waiter rubs at a glass with dirtied tea towel. He nods when I catch his eye. I know that he is an illegal immigrant with no passport, working for cash in hand. That is not my concern, a petty crime compared with the unreported stories that lie beneath the muddied surface of the dailies.

The café is quiet today the only slight disturbance was when that psychiatrist chap, Holiday, rushed in and sat with old Blumenfeld, the Jewish stamp collector. Blumenfeld is rarely excited but makes exception when discussing the price of gold, rare postage stamps and land stolen by Palestinians. Or Canaanites, as he calls them.

Having surveyed the human contents of the café, I glance back at the words before me: Hackney is a grand place for raising chickens. I have been waiting to see these words for more years than I can count; I had almost given up. This sedentary life, sipping cappuccinos and reading the newspapers in their entirety, had nearly bested me. Yes, me, Lionel Figgis, once a rising star of MI6! Make a mistake in MI6 and you get side-lined pretty quickly. The Fox Club rescued me from administrative obscurity.

Clearly Hackney is not a good place for raising chickens but I scratched my now grey head trying to recall the protocol and remember where I had left my revolver. Did I still have a parachute? Yes, I think it was stowed away in the back of the airing cupboard. Not that I could get the insurance to fly on a plane these days, especially with my heart condition. I was moved from official intelligence in '75. After a few months in Gibraltar I was seconded to B Division in most unusual circumstances, which I can't talk about here for reasons that usually end in death. Anyway, B Division no longer exists. It never really did – it was just a front for the Fox Club. I know you won't have heard of it. Very few people have and if they had they would deny it. But it exists, I tell you. I have been working for them since that hot summer of '76. The last active job I had for them was in '87. Two people died that day. It never made the news; Fox Club work rarely did. A lot of people went 'missing' in the '80s. Bad people; people with the wrong affiliations. You do not know the price paid to keep a country safe, to protect the truth.

Since then my job has been to wait for the code and initiate the protocol. Waiting requires patience and the gradual ability to dissolve into the mundaneness of life. You get used to it, especially if the coffee is good. So I waited. Freda, my wife, thought I was in Quality Assurance till '93. My second lie to her was that I was the President of the Black Cats Bowls Club. But the reality was that I just drank coffee and read the broadsheets. I am a whizz at the *Times* crossword, clues both quick and cryptic. I can advise you on the best ISAs in which to store your hard-earned money. I can discuss the unfairness of a working mother in a workplace hierarchy designed by men. I could probably predict who will win the next election and by how much, give or take a few seats. It's all in print you know. Add a truth to fiction and it eventually just sounds like the truth. Sell enough copies and everyone believes it. Anyone can be persuaded, so be careful what you write. Be careful what you read. I digress.

My memory was exceptional, now it is a little fuzzy, but the telephone number to initiate the protocol circles in my head like a cat chasing its tail.

I half-jog to the house, out of breath, fuelled by long-awaited excitement and caffeine. Ironically, Freda is boiling chicken bones when I return to the house, which leaves an unpleasant but reassuringly familiar aroma as I enter the hallway. I ascend the stairs two at a time, like I am twenty years younger.

I am cautious as the landline upstairs now seems dangerous, and I regret the careless complacency which led me to ditch the 'clean' phone back in '94. It was difficult to repair and, well, part of me never thought I would see this day. Training makes me think of my gun and I try to recall where I last placed it. I rummage around amongst handkerchiefs and loose keys in the drawer beneath my wardrobe. It isn't there but I locate it in the ottoman at the foot of the bed, buried amongst scratchy grey blankets and white cotton sheets. The small revolver I find locked in a wooden Havanan cigar box alongside ticket stubs from '66 and the letter my father wrote me before he died.

When I dial the number I can barely hear the dial tone because my heart beats loud in my now wheezy chest. The first two times no one picks up; the third time a female voice.

'Fontaine,' the voice answers. I feel light-headed and I can't remember what to say. What was the phrase?

'Hackney misplaced some chickens.'

'What?'

'Er . . . Hackney is a grand place for raising chickens.'

I feel the palpable silence as her mind is turning.

'Are you sure?' she says.

'Hackney is a grand place for raising chickens,' I repeat.

'Don't expect too many eggs.'

The phone receiver is replaced but I hear two clicks, not one. Two minutes later and Freda has ascended the stairs and the bedroom door is ajar as she stares down on me from the top of bi-focals. She can't see it from the door but the revolver now feels heavy and guilty in my lap.

'I'm not President of the Black Cats Bowls Club,' I say.

'Have you got another woman?' she is glaring, angry. I laugh at the absurdity. Has she not looked at me recently? I have grey hair sprouting from my nose and ears. My eyebrows now look like they have been knitted together!

'No!'

'Who is she? She sounds young.'

'Freda, don't be absurd! I'm a spy ... of sorts ... intelligence ... of sorts.'

'What?' she exclaims angrily.

'I work for the Prime Minister.' Do I still work for the Prime Minister? No contact for all these years, just regular payments wired anonymously.

'You're a bloody liar, Lionel!' she shouts at me.

'I'm serving my country.'

'You're a liar. Who is she?'

'Who?'

'The girl on the phone!'

'Er ... Fontaine? ... I don't know, I've never met her.'

'Liar!'

She stomps off like a child and I am reminded of all the things broken that I never fixed. It's me, Lionel, the man you married, I want to say, but there is just the emptiness of the open doorway. Blackwood always said that the Fox Club would be the death of me.

Fontaine (Elisabeth)

—— ❧ ——

I first met the journalist Alex Monroe when he interviewed my father nearly six months ago after a leak of B Division post-war files connected to political assassinations. A flurry of media activity led to misdirected speculation. It was clear that B Division did not exist on paper. The only connecting name was ex-government official, Sir Michael Fontaine, who was supposedly suffering from the beginnings of dementia. My father was always an excellent actor. President of Eton's Shakespeare Society in his day.

When the story gradually surfaced and hastily moved from the front page to page 7, the only person still researching the story two weeks later was Monroe. The day he used the phrase 'Fox Club' in a small article in the *Independent*, was the same day he died.

It is ironic that at the same time Monroe was researching the Fox Club, he was also working for me. I hired him. Freelancers are easily purchased for the right fee, especially journalists who are greedy for stories both real and imagined. I thought I could throw him off the Fox Club scent. I fed him a story that media tycoon, Develaire, was bribing politicians. I knew there was some truth in it because you rarely reach the top through honest living and integrity. It would have been a surprise to me if Develaire wasn't corrupt, and it was clear that he had picked his own man to rise to the top. Another puppet dangling loosely from the media's fickle string. So when I heard from a flustered Monroe that the Deputy Prime Minister would be killed in Norway at the weekend, it was with disbelief until I had to mop up at the airport. Sadly the Deputy PM was expendable in the grand scheme of things, but the safety of the Prime Minister is another matter entirely. The sudden loss of a Prime Minister leaves a vacuous hole which all manner of power-hungry politicians wish to step in to. Churchill knew this. What was it he said? Leaders must have conviction and calling, they must be transparent, not tainted by a lust for power.

Today I sent Stasia to the Tennyson building to review the crime scene surrounding the body of Alex Monroe. His death is on my hands and it seems clear that the killer is connected to Develaire. Stasia didn't call. Three hours is the time allowed to survey a scene, extract evidence and file an initial report. When she didn't pick up her phone, not even the personal line which I had used to monitor her social media interactions, I knew something was wrong.

When I pick the lock of the door to her flat I find Stasia's crumpled body on the wooden floor and a ginger cat resting on blood-stained paper, absently licking a four-toed paw.

'Stasia. Stasia!' I cry out, shaking her body, but the only response was the cat nudging my hand with soft, fur-lined cheek. I hesitate for a moment then make a call.

'Yes, hello?' the old familiar voice answers, sending conflicting memories and emotions I try to block out.

'I need you. Mendeleev is down and she's lost a lot of blood.'

'Who is this?'

'… it's me, Lizzie. Stasia's hurt and I need you.'

A pause.

'Fontaine, you know I'm not that kind of doctor anymore. What is her pulse?'

'Around 30.' Why did he have to be so clinical, so aloof? My father, always professionally distant, even with his children.

'Let her go, she's a complication. Stay focussed. The death of the Deputy Prime Minister is just the start of it, mark my words.'

'She's gonna die.'

'Let her go.' The conversation is over as the line is cut. My father, devoid of compassion or any apparent feeling. Cold like the surgeon's blade he used to wield. I want to remember that he is a man of duty, chosen. I want to reach into my past, grab hold of my training and remember that to function in the field you must detach yourself from emotion. But as I sit holding Stasia's limp hand, mentally imploring her pulse to go faster, I feel like crying and the stony wall my father placed around me begins to crumble. Stasia is so young and talented, how can I walk away? How can I let her slip slowly from the promise of this life? Her life. So I break protocol and call the ambulance using Stasia's civilian phone, and watch the paramedics from the other side of the street.

I bury my tears because now is not a time for weakness, but hours later I find myself at the hospital, standing over Stasia, who lies sleeping but stable. She looks so fragile; pale white skin disturbed by the invasiveness of plastic tubes. I can be clinical and precise but the sparse white room is devoid of anything personal and leaves me feeling nauseous with an over-riding feeling to flee. Even the colourful painting depicting a vase of flowers is trying too hard; it doesn't fit. I want the white walls to swallow it up and dispense with this lie.

I watch Stasia in the quietness of the isolated room. It surprises me that I have allowed myself to form this unspoken attachment to her. I sometimes think she is a better version of me. She has the potential not to fail; the potential to be happy.

Suddenly her head moves side to side erratically and I hear her pulse quicken through the monitor. She mumbles something incoherent in a dream-like state. Polish? Maybe Russian?

'Matka! Matka! I found her, Matka!'

I watch her thin lips forming shapes of words I do not know. And then her restlessness ceases. Her eyes look directly at me and she says, 'Samantha Just. The girl in the lift.' Then she disappears back inside her unconscious delirium.

Samantha Just.

Call this coincidence, but I know her; the pink-haired thief, an odd collector of strange items. Our paths crossed several months ago when she stole the Foreign Secretary's speech notes during a Conservative Party conference. The notes contained material that had been deemed too sensitive to divulge to such a wide audience. Now the PM was concerned with media repercussions; questions he didn't want answered.

That afternoon, on a hunch, I followed Samantha home from the conference. She didn't fit in with the Conservative crowd with her pink hair and long, silver-threaded socks. When I say 'home', it turned out to be a large office on the sixth floor of some *blue sky* marketing agency. I found the notes with a stack of papers from minor politicians, neatly residing on a well-ordered desk. Above them on a shelf, photograph albums lined up precisely in rows. Not one out of place.

'Why are you stealing these notes?' I ask.

'I collect adjectives,' she says seriously. And when I look through the paper sheets she holds before me, words are circled with red ink. *Inexpensive. Outstanding. Perfect.* I want to laugh but I sense for her there is nothing funny in this.

'What do you do here?' I say, looking around the office-cum-bedroom with its bean bags and floor cushions scattered next to a grey desk and cream futon.

'I collect things.'

'What things?'

'Photographs. Leaves. Other people's conversation; I write them in a notebook.'

I don't say anything, I just stare at her to see if she is telling the truth; there is no hint of deception in her voice. I was impressed that this street girl had managed to move into this office and set up home without anyone in the building suspecting any different. Those creative types haven't got any kind of boundaries or common sense. Fluffy work-shy chancers, my father used to say. I smile at the thought.

'How long have you been here?' I say.

'367 days.'

'Really?' I say, surprised.

'I told them downstairs I work for Head Office in Brussels. They believe I am working on a top secret government project to help market the Prime Minister. He is coming across a little grey.' And now she does laugh out loud. Her face creases uneasily as if reminded how to perform this rarely used action.

Now, when I arrive at the marketing agency, I bluff my way past reception using the power of simple words spoken with confidence. The door is wide open to Samantha's office and the floor of the once-ordered space is littered untidily with photographs and blood and glass. There is no sign of Samantha but I notice a pink-striped musette bag hanging next to a straw hat on a coat stand.

Inside the bag I find a letter from Monroe to his girlfriend. He has hidden evidence about the Fox Club in his flat. He knows everything!

I tried to contain him but he was much smarter than I ever gave him credit for. I must get that evidence. I must remain focussed and control this situation. What would my father do?

And the phone rings, breaking my train of thought, stalling me from decisions I need to make. I answer it on the third ring.

'Fontaine,' I say in answer.

'Hackney misplaced some chickens,' replies an out of breath, wheezy voice.

'What?'

'Er . . . Hackney is a grand place for raising chickens.'

'Are you sure?' I say unprofessionally. Despite the recent events I never really expected to hear this phrase.

'Hackney is a grand place for raising chickens,' the voice repeats.

'Don't expect too many eggs,' I reply, gathering my wits.

Who would have thought such ridiculous words could activate such an important protocol. Churchill always had a sense of humour.

Words

—⁓—

The editor told me to find 300 words. Visit the allotments in Hackney, he said, some local residents have been successfully keeping chickens and sharing the eggs within the community. A feel-good story. You need one occasionally to break up the pages of gloom and negativity and gossip.

This is a good assignment, a jolly. So I ride the tube and jump off early so I can walk in the sun. I smell the allotment before I see it. A scent of earth and greenery, maybe a whiff of onions floating under the toxic trail of leaded fumes. Yes, I feel the words forming even before I arrived at the wired gate. A gate flanked by tall, unruly weeds and a scattering of brown wooden huts lovingly created from scrounged timber, corrugated iron and broken pallets.

The old boy in the dusty grey suit had missing teeth and smoked a rollie through nicotine-stained hands. He laughed, loud and long, and with a wide, open grin.

'No chickens 'ere son, foxes ad 'em all or maybe the Poles. When they're not fishing the River, of course.'

'Will you be receiving some more?'

'Nah.'

'What do you grow here?'

'Carrots. Loads of 'em.'

Foxes eat chickens. Some feel-good story! But it wasn't all bad; the old boy wanted to chat and pulled out some stripy frayed deck chairs that smelled like manure. And I listened to his life story and day dreamed in the sun, sitting on the deck chairs drinking bottles of Mackeson's that emerged from a shed, creatively engineered from asbestos sheets and decking. After five bottles I wrote the short article, *Hackney is a grand place for raising chickens,* which was about everything and nothing and is quite probably the best piece I will ever write.

Newbridge (Junior Reporter)

The Stranded Fox

—— ෙ ා ——

*A fox is never stranded it chooses to be alone, walking unmarked trails
with the freedom of an animal that has no natural predator.*

I scavenge by day as freely as I do by night. Every hour is mine. I own
your city; every street and garden; every allotment is my home. I am
not afraid of you. You watch me, you ignore me and you do nothing.
You pretend you don't see me like when you cross the road from the
malodorous men who live in sleeping bags, begging for coins with
dirty hands and vacant, unseeing eyes. My eyes see everything; my
ears hear every sound. I am the urban wolf and I am not afraid. But I
am afraid of the man in black; he has the air of the devil. I watch him
now, from safe distance, as I sit on the warm bonnet of a rusting blue
Nova. When I hear him speak, his words carried by the wind, I fear he
has no soul, or if he does, it is corrupted beyond repair. I cannot sense
any good in him.

My instinct is to run, to escape the oppressive atmosphere that
closes in on me. But I am held there, spellbound, transfixed by the
calmness of his voice – it is almost musical. A song I do not want to
sing. But the words do not match his tone. How can you order death
so subtly and with no apparent feeling?

'He is moose hunting tomorrow. It is better for him to *remain* in
Norway.'

Twilight is an odd time. A disparity between day and night. A crossing
of borders. I hide in twilight and catch vermin with the deception of
light, so why wouldn't the man in black conduct his business in this
unclear space.

His car is black and expensive, but he is too important to drive. The
tall man with the wide-brimmed hat, who is part chauffeur, part

dispatcher of souls, sits behind the wheel with tight leather gloves more suited to strangling than to aid driving. The devil talks in a hushed singsong voice, with open clear words that dispatch orders that are to be followed, not questioned.

They think they are alone in these grey acres of empty tarmac as dusk begins to set in, but I watch them carefully and hear every word, as does the man in the yellow skip, who has sat patiently for hours, waiting to catch this moment. I sense him. He is quiet but I hear him. I hear his nervous breath, the scratch of his pencil as he makes hasty factual notes on lined paper. I heard the whir of the camera video, though to you it has no sound. Your eyes have made your other senses weak.

When the devil is gone my heart begins to rest and I listen for the call of the vixens on heat. I am distracted but I do not forget what I have seen or the feeling of dread that held me immovable. I briefly wonder whether the man in the skip felt like this. Whether he too, is afraid to move. You humans fear much. I have seen it consume you and prevent you moving forward. Fear cripples you and suddenly you are old and it is too late to live out your dreams or be the best version of yourself you could have been. Take my advice: to live is to walk through fear boldly.

Men are not like animals. Your spirits long for the light but darkness pursues you with a desire to destroy. I do not envy you the complexity of a long life.

As I walk off into the night, I turn to take one last look and watch the man jump from the skip, pink-striped musette bag swinging gently, and hope that he has what it takes to complete the task God has put before him.

Fletch

When I first discovered the fox I was already stranded. But I wasn't alone. The broken girl sat close but out of reach with words beyond poetry.

I would watch the street-weathered fox run along the ageless wall that Papa, Jack and I took down one hot day in August. Brick dust and heat hung in the air accompanied by Merlin engines flying east in blue, cloudless skies. Three sets of eyes; father to son.

From that day the fox was always there, on the edge of my vision, in the small hours of pale morning light or the darkness of sleepless night, when stars sat scattered in every direction from the moon.

When I stopped chasing dreams all that remained were the undiluted words and the Holy Spirit which guided my ink. Words formed from memories and life, and books with forgotten titles and conversations with the broken girl who listened to who I was and searched for who I am. Conversations about everything and nothing. And God; God is in the detail and it is detail that makes everything whole.

When I look back she is in every story and page, just as clearly as she became part of me; unconsciously. She found me instantly, but I was always there, in the mirror, reflecting back at her.

During those summers in the sun, the confident fox cubs would play with a tennis ball thrown around with playful feet, just like the ball that I threw to Jack as we discussed ideas and words and the Word. And I gave everything of myself and all the knowledge and wisdom I had acquired these last years. In fact, everything I had learned in all my years, because only a fool does not learn from mistakes and life.

Where I was going then was clear. God gives clarity when you have obedience and intention and peace.

Like the fox I sometimes did not sleep, but arose in the early hours to escape endless thinking without action. Thinking without action leads to confusion. And eventually death.

I held confusion at bay, nurtured but at arm's length. One day the thin cord that held it there broke and I let it go like a balloon slipping from a child's hand. But the string that held my balloon was wire and it cut my hand as I held on with futility.

When I let go all that finally prevailed was the Word and the broken girl, as I desperately held on to the boy with questions with one hand tightly.

Driving with Blackwood

The mourners watch me with bewildered silence as I close the lid on the coffin and walk away through the church gate, with one eye on the dog sleeping beneath the tree. It seems untroubled with shallow breathing, blissfully unaware.

A rusting blue car at the end of the field is waiting with the engine running. When I peer through the open window I see that despite the heat the driver is wearing a brown coat and green military beret. He salutes me with liver-spotted hand.

'Lieutenant Blackwood at your service,' he says.

'Can you drive me, Blackwood?' I say, hoarsely.

'Of course, sir, get in.'

The passenger seat is worn and it takes two sharp yanks to make the seat belt work, but I finally click it into place. It is only then that it occurs to me how much my feet ache and how far I have walked these last few days. As Blackwood moves off I look in the wing mirror. The image that looks back at me is dishevelled, barely recognisable from the man who slept in the church. The bruise on my head is darker now and the once-white shirt is browned with blood and dirt, the front pocket ripped, hanging loosely.

We sit in silence. I think of Samantha and the relief in her voice when I told her where her daughter is. She trusted me, accepted my word. I never gave Blackwood directions but he drives along happily around bendy country roads, whistling quietly between his teeth.

'Sorry about the radio,' he says, pointing at the dashboard. 'Jammed on Radio 3 and the cassette thingamajig is broken. Not that keen on opera anyway.'

'Where are you driving?' I say.

'Top secret. Fox Club business.' And he taps his nose with his index finger.

I smell the sea long before we reach the coast. The salty air ruffles my hair as I lean with one arm out the window. Black-headed seagulls fly above me. We're running on empty, the red needle way past zero, but Blackwood seems content to just bimble along at fifty.

I see the storm approaching in the cracked wing mirror, a gathering of black rain clouds fronted by a large black car with headlights beaming. I sense the oppressive darkness of it, the speed of its approach. Blackwood senses it too.

'Hello. Trouble,' he says in classic British understatement, taking a long gaze into his rear-view mirror. 'Don't worry, lad. I had advanced vehicle training in the Airborne. Lorries mainly.' And he grips the wheel tighter and places his foot down heavy on the accelerator. I never knew a 1.2L Nova could reach 100mph but shuddering and smoking it did, and Blackwood swerves around corners with the black vehicle almost touching bumpers and flashing lights.

A long-barrelled gun takes aim. Two shots. One blowing the driver's side rear tyre; the second, a bullet through the rear window and into Blackwood's beret covered head. And as I watch Blackwood slump over the steering wheel, we skid at high speed, smashing through a wooden fence, coming to a crashing halt as metal meets rock and the blue Nova sits precariously close to the grassy cliff edge. I pull the handbrake. Instinct.

I try to open the door but it is pushed closed with a large boot. The owner, a man wearing a wide-brimmed hat, pushes the muzzle of a long-barrelled gun through the window.

'Mr. Develaire wants to speak with you.' And the shadowy figure from the video, Develaire, stands before me, clothed in black whilst the rain from the approaching storm catches up, soaking into the expensive threads. Black suit, black shirt, black tie. His face is pale and pasty from the absence of natural light. His grooming is immaculate, not a hair out of place, and his cologne reaches me quickly like cordite from a fuse. He has the air of ageing hidden by money.

Develaire steps forward and a feeling beyond despair takes hold of me, an invisible tight fist around my throat. It's difficult to describe but I know that I am more afraid of Develaire than his henchman's gun. I look for ways to escape, but even as I look at Blackwood's corpse blocking an available exit I know that to open this door would be to fall off the edge of a cliff. Trapped.

'I just want to talk,' Develaire says smoothly, 'You can't remember your name, can you?' It is rhetorical, not a question to be answered.

'I could tell you your name. I just want Monroe's memory card.'

'I don't have it,' I say.

'We both know you do. What do you want? Money? The girl?'

I look at him and know that he speaks of Samantha. How does he know?

'Samantha Just. You like her, don't you.'

I say nothing.

'She wouldn't like you if she really knew you.'

'She's my friend,' I say defensively.

'Her baby is missing because of you. You killed her adoptive parents. Yes, you killed them. Killed them with your car.'

'No,' I say with unbelief, but as I put my hand to the bruise on my head I know it's true. I remember rolling as the Volkswagen tumbled around and around. I see their bodies twisted and dead. Broken limbs.

'No!'

'Yes. You did it.'

'It was an accident!'

'Was it? I can help you. I have influence. Connections. I work inside circles that can't be seen. I have enough wealth to buy every judge. You can walk free! No jail time. Give me the memory card.'

'I don't have it,' I say, but I sense it inside my pocket.

'You lie. I know you have it. Why go through any pain? Give up. Give it up. My friend here can kill you quick or torture you for hours. The tools of torment lie within easy reach.' He looks over at his vehicle. 'Just give it over and walk free.'

'I can't,' I say. Despite the fear inside of me I know God has brought me this far.

'I know you are a man of God. You have principles,' he says, reading my mind.

'God told me where to find Samantha's baby,' I say truthfully.

'Did he really? You are deluded. Even if he did exist, why would he speak to someone like you, a killer? You've had too much sun, not enough to drink – you're hallucinating. Come in and rest in my car. We can take you to the hospital, get you cleaned up. There's a nasty bruise on your head. You've probably got a head injury. You've been in two car crashes now. It's not God speaking, it's just in your head.'

'Samantha needs me,' I say, but the words begin to sound hollow in my own ears.

'Does she? You can't help her from prison. That's where you will go for killing Penny and Stephen. I can make sure you stay free. Free from jail, just give me the memory card. You can't help her.'

Penny. Stephen. I can feel my resolve disintegrating at the sound of their names. Why would Samantha trust me? She spoke to me for months and I could never say a word in reply. I don't even know my name! I reach inside my shirt pocket and hand over the memory card, and as I do the man with the long-barrelled gun pushes me and the car over the cliff edge, the handbrake giving way to his ample body weight.

As the car gathers momentum and launches off the cliff, the gathering storm overtakes me, showering me with hail like bullets from a machine gun. Swirling wind and pelting rain hit me as blue sky is blotted out by grey and black clouds, and as the car nose dives in mid-air I am pressed up against the windscreen. The faulty seat belt gives way and the bonnet cuts into choppy waves like a knife into butter. Despair lurks within the murky greyness and although the seawater is cold I black out.

In my mind I swim through the blackness. It is thick and soupy and difficult to navigate. A delicate hand holds mine and I cling to Samantha, knowing that without her, death will claim me.

'You're a failure,' I hear Develaire whisper. 'And a murderer.' And as we watch a re-run of me driving a car into Penny and Stephen, Samantha's hand slowly slips from mine and any remaining hope is blotted out with despair. I hear Samantha shout, 'Amelia!' as a little girl with bunches runs passed me until she is blurry and out of focus.

'Why, God? I did what you said! Don't leave me!' I shout angrily.

An hour later I am awoken by intense light entering the windscreen. It is warm and bright and comforting and penetrates my closed eyelids with a bright pinkness that reminds me of summer days asleep in the garden. I taste the salt on my lips and open one eye to find Blackwood's corpse slumped over the wheel, sea water up to my knees, and a crab moving across my lap.

The children who discover me wear frayed jean shorts and run through the wet sand with pirate challenges and bare feet. Huzzah!

'Hey, mister – hey mister, are you alright?' They knock on the window, oblivious to the corpse. Maybe they think Blackwood is sleeping. Young faces with curly hair and carefree, mischievous eyes look through the glass. A young boy reaches through and touches my arm. There are about twelve of them, all heavily tanned, with wild hair and a feral glint in their eyes. The tallest child's badge of rank is a red baseball cap worn backwards, and he moves through the sea to take a closer look at what the storm has thrown up.

'That was some storm, mister,' he says in croaky, half-broken tones.

'Yes,' I manage to reply.

'You're gonna need our help,' he says. A statement of intent, and he wades off, only to return five minutes later with a length of strong blue rope. He loops it around the remaining bumper, calling out orders, to the others who obey him without question. The door is jammed so I climb out the car window and pick up the rope too. Together we tug at the blue Nova until it is out of the sea and onto shingle. Grey-green seawater leaks from every opening and hole; it gushes onto the sand.

'There you go,' he says smiling, 'good job we are not charging today.'

'Thanks,' I say, not sure what I should do with it now.

'Try the ignition.'

'I think it is a little wet,' I say in understatement, looking at seaweed still floating in the back.

'It will dry out.'

The unbelief in my face doesn't need words. He reads me and says:

'Nothing is impossible. Have a little faith.' And with that he runs off and they all peel away, following him like he was some important General or Arabian Prince. I watch their footprints forming in the sand as they run along the sunny beach, shadowed cliff edge towering overhead. All that remained of the sudden storm was a line of drying black seaweed, the occasional jellyfish and sea-smoothed driftwood. I open the driver's door and look at the slumped body of poor old Blackwood. Who was he and what is Fox Club business? It gets you killed, that's all I know.

Blackwood's right hand rests with thumb and fingers on the ignition key. I pull the frailness that is his body from the driver's seat, with the boy's last words reverberating inside me. I am dry and empty; all feeling has gone. The Still Small Voice is now silent. But I have His Word and hear my father's voice say, 'Nothing is impossible with God,' and I mouth it silently like I did as a child.

God started this, so I turn the key, clutching on to the little faith that the boy has restored in me. The engine splutters into life on the third turn.

Prime Minister

꧁꧂

Appleby told him to look sombre. He hadn't liked Jeffrey much but there was no mistaking he was an excellent politician, especially during the rather awkward European exit. It was a shame they had never been friends. But there wasn't time, only politics, and now he was dead.

Appleby had suggested a black tie today. A little early he thought, but Appleby likes subtle visual effect. He said that the nation was still mourning the untimely death of Caplin; the nation needed to see their leader was emotionally sensitive, but not weak. So as I order more stealth attacks on terrorist strongholds in the Middle East with one intake of breath, I also exhale a sad, thoughtful expression when 'officially' told the news that poor Jeffrey has been shot. The cameras are eager to capture both emotions and I briefly ponder the sad fact that it may have been more useful to have received acting classes than a doctorate in politics.

After addressing the nation, I listen to the ripple of post-speech chatter as Appleby ushers me into the car and releases me from further questions.

'I've just lied to the nation, Appleby.'

'It had to be done, Mr. Prime Minister.'

'Did it?'

'If the public discover the Deputy PM was assassinated in the same week as the death of Frank Caplin, our country would struggle with the instability. The economy is already diving again, sir. We don't need another hit.'

'Yes, yes, I know. And every available resource has been assigned to apprehend the killer? We need to know who is behind this.'

'Yes, sir.'

'I don't want this dragging on. It's making me nervous. Making my wife nervous.'

'I could send around a physician, sir?'

'She doesn't need a bloody doctor! She needs to know that she won't wake up tomorrow and find out that she's a widow! I need to know it, dammit!'

'Sir, we have doubled your security detail. Postponed unnecessary trips.'

'Sorry, Appleby, this whole week is getting to me. Losing Jeffrey has put me under a lot of pressure, especially now Caplin is dead. The media is already naming that buffoon, Francis Glib, as his replacement. If that idiot gets voted in, we might as well have the media running the country!'

'You still think he is Develaire's man?'

'I'm sure of it.'

The church comes into view and I see the Priest waiting by large wooden doors that are ornately decorated with metalwork, finished in matt black. Beautiful curled hinges and weathered oak.

'Do I have to do this, Appleby?' I say.

'Sir, we have been through this, the nation needs to see their leader conversing with God during sad and difficult times.'

'And it's been fully checked to ensure complete safety?'

'I personally oversaw it, sir.'

I feel relief. I trust Appleby, which is good because I see him more than my wife.

The Priest welcomes me with a firm handshake and reassuring eyes as flashes from photographers light up the scene. When I enter the foyer the doors are shut, and I welcome the peaceful silence as I walk along the central aisle and smell the polished wooden pews and burning candle wax. There is a serene quality to the inside of churches, especially old ones. In my busyness I forgot this. Maybe God hasn't abandoned us.

'Do you want to light a candle, Mr. Prime Minister?' asks the Priest, snapping me away from my thoughts.

'Sorry?'

'Light a candle. For the Deputy Prime Minister.'

'Er ... yes. Will it help?'

'It is good to remember the dead, but...' He leaves the sentence hanging but the rope is short.

'But?' I question, tugging with both hands on the offered wisdom.

'But it is better to remember the living.'

I look at him and see beyond the robes of church office. There is no false piety; there is studied intelligence – a lightness about him that is difficult to place. He looks peaceful, dare I say it. We light the candle in silence and I mutter a prayer of loosely attached words and unconsciously look up, hopeful that God might be hovering just above me.

'Have you always been a priest?' I ask him, to break the silence.

'No, sir. I worked the Stock Market until it broke me. I found God when I stopped chasing money.' He laughs in a wooden, clunky way, and it is clear that it is no joke.

'Money has a nasty habit of controlling us,' I say, thinking of recent resignations by minor politicians; greed playing on both sides of the fence.

'You can't serve both God and money,' the Priest says.

'Matthew 6:24,' I say. 'Catholic school,' I say in answer to his raised eyebrows.

There's a gap in the conversation, which I try to fill.

'Who do you serve?' I say.

'I serve God and my country,' he replies seriously. 'Most of the time they are compatible.'

It is now I that raise my eyebrows, but I remain silent.

I look around at the beauty of the stained-glass windows and well-chiselled grey brick. The ornately carved wood of pews in their perfect lines.

'I like it here; the quietness. Out there I am bombarded by a thousand voices. It is difficult to know which ones to listen to.' I say.

'Discernment is difficult to come by.' The Priest holds my gaze and I wonder whether wisdom could find its place in my Cabinet.

'Are you discerning?'

'Only when I listen to God.'

He walks off and through a small white door to the right of the altar.

'Er . . . , what do I do now?' I shout, but he has gone.

I look around and the church is deserted, just the darkened empty entrance and the black dog of the media waiting behind it with snarling teeth. Even Appleby has evaporated. In the emptiness I notice the flicker of light streaming through the stained-glass window. It scatters playful colours across the starkness of grey stone floors. Blues and reds; greens and yellows. What was it that Churchill said? *All the colours come back into picture.*

Outside the white door I hear voices debating in hushed tones. As I enter I stumble over a bundle of green velour curtains that lie on the floor. Beyond it, to my surprise I see the Priest and Appleby huddled together, listening to a woman who I vaguely recognise.

'What's going on, Appleby?' I say, irritated, wondering how he entered this room so stealthily. But he doesn't reply. The girl steps forward and holds out a hand, which I do not shake.

'Do you remember me, sir?'

'You're Michael Fontaine's daughter, aren't you?'

'Yes.'

'What do you want?' I ask her the question but I am glaring at Appleby, who remains uncharacteristically quiet.

'The Fox Club protocol has been initiated, sir,' she says.

'Fox Club?' I say with a feigned puzzled look.

'Don't deny knowledge, sir. It's been activated and we need to get you safe.'

There is a long silence as I look at Fontaine.

'You don't become Prime Minister by running. A Prime Minister doesn't hide!'

'It's just temporary, while we neutralise the threat. Surely you don't believe that it is coincidence that Caplin and the Deputy PM should die in the same week?'

No I didn't, I was waiting for a bullet with my name on it.

'Who's going to run the country in my absence?' In answer to my question a figure steps from the shadows with an old, familiar, lopsided grin.'

'Hey, cousin,' the man says with an oily smile.

'Layton! You are supposed to be hiding out in Venezuela!'

'I have come back to save the day,' he says, still smiling that

106

ridiculous smile. And I wonder whether he is still hooked on amphetamines.

'Fontaine, he can't be trusted. The man's a bloody crook; wanted in at least three South American countries. And ours! The nation thinks he is dead,' I say loudly. '*The nation thinks he is dead,*' I repeat quietly.

'Exactly,' says Fontaine, 'He is unique, Mr. Prime Minister. He is the spitting image of you, sir – you could be twins. And the world thinks he is dead.'

'You plan to swap me? Preposterous!'

'My father revised the protocol when you came into power. It is a good plan, sir, and I recommend we follow it.'

Layton has an unusually wide skillset and by the time he has slipped into my suit he is strutting around, mimicking my walk and expressions with uncanny accuracy.

'I want to be pardoned for my part in this,' he says with a grin, and Appleby and the Priest lead him away by the arm, muttering last minute instructions. Layton definitely hasn't got a doctorate, but he can act.

Much later, when the Priest goes for tea, I take a nap in the cold stone vestry, wrapped in green velour curtains, sharing oxygen with an abundance of spiders and the occasional carefree mouse.

Assassin (2)

The woman sits next to me, painfully breathing in and out, holding her extended stomach, but my thoughts are on Develaire. I can't be late for the drop off even if I have nothing to give. Develaire has no time for failure; his displeasure is something you would not pursue.

The bike messenger's camera was empty; no memory card; no evidence. My first thoughts were of the girl with pink hair. I sensed there was something different about her; the unspoken guild of thieves knows one of their own. Pickpockets share their own code but despite that, I should have shot her when I had the chance. Corpses are easier to search, they move less.

When I approached the Tennyson building for the second time that day I watched the Polish student, Mendeleev, vacate by the rear entrance. Rather than returning to the scene of my crime I followed her on instinct.

Develaire said that the Fox Club were on to him.

'The Fox Club?' I say.

'The name keeps resurfacing,' he says, 'linked to an undocumented protocol.' He mutters something about Winston Churchill. In his face, I see the tiny beginnings of paranoia, a chink in his armour. He shows me a picture of Elisabeth Fontaine. Serious blue eyes and a floaty ponytail.

'She's connected,' he says.

'Connected to what?' I say.

'The Fox Club, weren't you listening, dammit!' he says, exasperated.

I don't know what this Fox Club is and I don't think Develaire does either. That's what worries him.

Back in my car the pregnant woman moans next to me, labour pains intermittently pulsing through her body.

'Are we nearly there?' she says through gritted teeth.

'What is your name?' I say, trying to distract her.

'Hope,' she says, 'Ww ... why do you have a gun?' She looks at me sideways.

'I work for the government.' Lies fall from my lips so easily they sound like the truth.

'Doing what ... aaahh!' Her hands hold tightly around her extended stomach.

'I can't talk about it.' But it doesn't matter because the pain she experiences resurges in ever closer waves and we finish the drive to the hospital, in a silence punctuated only by painful sobs.

She leans in close as I support her delicate body into the hospital and the baby arrives in double time in a room with one nurse and a midwife. And I can't leave; her fingers are so tightly bound to mine that to wrench them now would hurt her. This is what happens when you start to care, when you give of yourself. You get connected and it is difficult to pull away.

I watched her tears and felt her pain in the sharp nails that dug into my hand. I was not prepared for the beautiful intensity of new life. The baby was small and pink and perfect. I looked on as it breathed its first lungful of oxygen. Its first cry in realisation that she has been removed from the safety of her mother's womb.

'What is it?' she says to me.

I can't speak. There are no words in my mouth. Just the thickness of unexpected emotion barely contained.

'A girl,' I finally breathe in almost silent whispered breath. 'It's a girl, Hope.'

'Thank you,' she says smiling. And the baby lies on her chest. I touch the sparse hair on her head and lean forward instinctively to smell her. This is life, I think.

That amazing baby smell lies deep within me. It is still on my hands as I try and take in what just happened. How did I become part of it? Despite the pain, Hope seemed so content. I have never seen happiness so tangible. I didn't know.

When I walk along the hospital corridor I don't notice people moving past me. I don't see their grey exteriors and sad faces, but I do notice the flowers in the gift shop. The orange petals are oval and perfect in their natural uniformity, and they have a scent. They smell of the morning and I buy them for Hope with the change in my pocket. *A day of firsts.*

I snap out of this thoughtful daydream the instant I bump head-on into Fontaine. I have never seen her in the flesh but there is no doubt in my mind it is her. My only thought now is that if I could bring her to the drop off, I wouldn't have failed. I would have something to give. I could use my favourite tweezers to extract information. We could unmask the Fox Club.

'You!' she says, on intake of breath. And I thrust the flowers into her face, the orange petals flutter down and the yellow stamens leave a sticky stain on her cheeks and nose, and she sneezes quickly while putting her hands up in defence. But I push her through an open door with such force that she falls over the still occupant of the single bed. And she is up, wielding a crutch straight at my head – I parry it with my left wrist, ignoring the throbbing sting. And she throws a glass. It smashes on my face with such a force that I feel the glass cut in. Jagged edges. And then her hands, fast and precise, attack me aggressively and it is clear that my overbearing size does not frighten her. Her moves are so fast that I wonder which school she was taught at; which Master? Dee Chin springs to mind by the way her wrists flick, or maybe the American, Chad Stevens.

And we fight hand to hand at the end of the bed while an old man sleeps in drugged morphia. His radio plays loudly and, absurdly, a duet between Julie Andrews and Dick van Dyke harmonises while I manage to grab Fontaine's wrist and fling her across the room. But she is quick to recover and a large Ming vase of questionable dynasty flies through the air. And as I duck she is through the open window and gone, as shards of blue and white china litter the floor. I gaze out between thin linen curtains moving gently in the wind and I see her hanging from a metal railing, blonde ponytail now loose, legs swinging. Before she jumps into the alley below she looks back and I see the bruise already forming around her left eye. She's gone before I have time to reach for my gun and I rue the chance I had to end her.

I sit on the bed and listen to the shallow breathing of the occupant. I don't look at him, but I smell his oldness. I see it in the beige dressing gown folded on the chair; in the grey, checked slippers on the floor. A greeting card depicting a Spitfire in mid-flight sits on the table. '*You are the best of me. Elsie xx*' scrawled inside in untidy blue biro. I don't look at him. I envy his age, his wrinkles; his obvious long life. I don't look at him, I look at my knuckles, grazed and flecked with Fontaine's blood; and hidden beneath, the silver scars of skirmishes long forgotten.

Is it nearly over? Will I really die at 40? If I could live, what an absurdity to think that I could change. That I could have a family. That I could be loved; by a woman.

When I return to the maternity ward, Hope sleeps peacefully but exhausted, with dried mascara on her cheeks. She looks content in her exhaustion; satisfied.

'Beautiful, isn't she,' says the nurse gazing at the baby. I didn't see her enter the room because my eyes were transfixed on thin red lips sucking a tiny pink fist.

'She's perfect,' I say.

Before I walk out the door I wipe my eyes on loosened shirt sleeves and leave the diamond cufflinks next to the bed. I like the way they sparkle; I always did.

Henderson (deceased) (2)

———— ❧ ————

As my soul drifted the sun gently burnt away the fog, and the pain I felt dissolved, as did time in the visceral space I now reside in. Time has no meaning here. There is no end and the beginning is so far behind me, I can't see it. The memories of living are already starting to fade.

When I lived I sat in the reassuring confines of my days. Thirteen thousand six hundred and seventy one days to be exact. There is a time for almost anything when you are alive, and everything appears possible when boundaries are blurred and existence is fuelled by an excess of money.

As I recall, the struggle for oxygen on this last day was the same as on the day of my birth. Oxygen. Starved of it, my mother said. I was a baby without a cry. Blue and limp and rushed from womb to the emergency ward in the first few seconds of my pitiful life. Maybe that is why I didn't bond with my mother. A loss of closeness; separation brought on by tubes and the fabricated necessity of incubators. Is that why I sought the touch of skin so fervently? Pursued it? It was this and the easy ignition of my anger that saw me put two men in hospital, followed closely by a short spell in a detention centre. All this before my eighteenth birthday.

Patterns of petty crime and periods of isolation are difficult to break. The girl who rescued me from my rapid decline needed a project and we built a life that was at times idyllic. I remember the day we picnicked by the river: the sun shone; I could only see her. But the things of the past haunted me. Suppressed anger spills into the good and pollutes it. And the touch of her skin disappeared faster than the blood that dried on my knuckles. I walked away from my life; a ghost. Unseen.

The dog I discovered the same day I found my father. It was stuck in the marshes, coated in mud. Three hours it took to reach and bring to shore. There was quite some crowd watching. When I washed it off, to my surprise it was black with white patches. It stuck to me like glue. My father scowled at me, 'What are you doing with that second-hand dog?' he said. We never spoke again. His image faded like the shadow he was in my life. A shadow on a cloudy day.

There was a time to kill and I found it with the sharp serrated edge of a bread knife. The crimes I committed after that were calculated and planned, so by the time **they** found me I was rough around the edges but gifted. I practised skills that satisfied my resurging anger and beneath the surface of normal society, my ability to track a man or lay explosives became legendary.

I embraced my mother before she died and wept tears of regret. Regret that she had not loved me harder. Regret that I had not told her I loved her. But the silence and the tears and the loss of what I had were all meaningless.

Now life has been stripped from me. I search for the memories of what made me happy, pushing past the bloody images of corpses; all the people I killed. Some like Riley I remember, some are faceless and devoid of obvious humanity. Anise is just a ghost in what remains of my mind. I search and search for her, remembering my hands upon her hips and the way I felt when she smiled. When she looked at me.

When I reach the beach I sense something is wrong, but can't put my finger on it. The quality of light is different, like the sun has been smothered. I hear Anise's voice but when I reach the wooden hut it is empty. I look through the window and see two quarters of an orange drying on a plate. A sea of ants march across the white china, waiting to consume the sticky juices. But Anise is absent. My hopeful call remains unanswered.

El Filosofo has been dragged up the beach. I am happy to see it. The boat's shabby perfection is a pleasure to look at, as are the memories it conjures up. So with haste I drag it to the sea, its pointy wooden hull drawing a line in the sand amongst seaweed and discarded crab shells. I look distantly out to sea as I hop into the floating vessel; it's odd but I cannot see the sparkle on the surface. I search for my rod and am pleased to find it resting comfortably in its usual place. The bait box I prise open, to find decaying maggots rotting alongside others striving to live. I place one on the hook and wait patiently, surprised by the absence of sea birds. It occurs to me that you could wait for ever when time has dissolved, so with a spark of impatience I peer over the side of the boat. Bile rises warm in my throat. The sea is blood! A deep red that laps against the side, stinking of dead fish that rise to the surface with limp tails and silver herringbone scales. Tarnished bodies. Single fish eyes look up at me accusingly. Horrified I hide in the bottom of the boat, my eyes consuming the grey skies, trying to rid myself of this sickly image.

The boat drifts and the fog returns and forms layers of grey that rise off the water and meet the sky in an expanse of nothingness. And I close my eyes to hide from the emptiness.

I am awoken by the sound of wood knocking on stone. A rippling tide gently pushes *El Filosofo* back and forth against a high wall built of stones that are bigger than several men could move. A rope ladder hangs within easy reach and I grab for its steps, itching to escape the bloody water. Over my shoulder I watch the boat gradually float away.

The ladder is high and at the top a room full of books. I am sure it is a library because I hear whispering in hushed voices; detached words and unfinished sentences that surround books of all shapes and sizes and various degrees of aging. Spines in blues and reds; greens and yellows; gold leaf writing in an unknown script; a shelf of oversized books with colourful dust jackets. The air doesn't move here and I sense the turning of pages in the palpable stillness. A stillness interrupted by the beat of my heart. Why does my heart still beat? Am I not dead?

The librarian turns the pages: a man in a roll-neck sweater, whose grey eyes study the book with apparent intentionality while he sits at a table amongst yellow parchment and ink stamps.

'Hello, Henderson,' he says without looking up.

'Where am I?' I say apprehensively.

'I think we both know that answer, Henderson.' He inclines his head towards two doors that lay before me. Thick brown oak with black ornate hinges. Side by side they stand.

'I suggest you just go through, Henderson. There is nothing further you can do. You had your time.'

'I've just been killed. I never finished my life.'

'You were 37. That is long enough.'

'Long enough!'

'Yes. Long enough to make a difference. Long enough to live beyond what is in front of you.'

'Bbbb . . . bbut I didn't know,' I stutter.

'The signs are everywhere. Did you not wake every morning and walk out into the light each day? Did you not sleep under a billion different stars?'

I nod unwillingly and he guides me by the elbow with strong calloused hands to the wide door. I push at it with reluctant, trembling fingers, and the darkness unfolds before me. Taking one last backward glance I watch the librarian leafing through a dog-eared copy of *Macbeth*. And the light that streams through the keyhole of the narrow door adjacent is so warm and bright that every part of me aches for it, knowing that without it, I do not exist.

Delphine

———&⁊———

The gunfire had become erratic and increasingly distant, but the smell of smoke still drifted in the air. The farmhouse door remained open just as the Colonel had left it as his worn boots strode through confidently. She felt an urge to shut the door and keep the warmth in, but continued to dig next to what remained of the vegetable garden. A couple of withered potatoes she found, and cleaning the soil off roughly, the girl buried them hastily in the confines of her brown jacket.

It wasn't until the young French girl began to move Saunier's body that she heard the engine of the jeep and crouched down with a Sten gun poised at the ready. When the Willy's jeep pulled up she half expected to see Churchill again. Had he changed his mind and now wanted to say a few words over Saunier's lifeless body? But no, it wasn't Churchill. From the passenger seat a big man with a large smile and a full brown-grey beard jumped down in fatigues, armed with a pen. His eyes surveyed the scene and took in the Sten gun aimed at his chest. He held out the pen and pointed.

'I'm unarmed,' he said.

I look from the bearded man in front of me to the fresh earth I had dug, and wish the hole was not another grave.

'You want a hand with that?' the man said, his head inclined towards Saunier's dead body. He is still smiling and doesn't wait for an answer. Scooping up Saunier's corpse like a sack of potatoes, he slings him into the newly dug grave.

'Careful, monsieur, that is an 'ero of France!' I say.

'Then why are you burying him next to potatoes!' he replies and lets out a booming laugh. These Americans fight well but have few manners. They often surprise me. The bearded man surprised me when he grabs a shovel from the jeep and lays the damp earth respectfully over Saunier's cold body. I tearfully watch the familiar

116

long grey moustache gradually disappearing and wipe my eyes with my red neckerchief.

'Quel est votre nom?' he says, handing me his hip flask after I offer up a prayer for my comrade with near silent breath.

'Delphine. Et vous?'

'Papa,' he says offering his hand before hopping back in the jeep.

'Where are you heading, monsieur?' I say.

'Next stop Paris!' he booms gaily, raising his hip flask in mock celebration. His jeep driver cheered; another big American who watched Papa intently.

'With a pen?' I say.

'Where there are guns and bodies, there is always a story,' he says.

'That is true.'

'The liberation of Paris is a long-awaited story.'

'I have an intriguing story, Monsieur,' I say, and he looks at me in such a way that I know he is already hooked. And I recount the previous few hours and tell of Winston Churchill captured by the German Colonel. The Colonel who released him after killing two SS officers. When I have finished his curious brown eyes search mine for the truth of it.

'Winston Churchill was held hostage in that farmhouse?' he says frowning, pointing at the grey brick house with the open door. I nod. He hops out the jeep and walks into the farmhouse. I hear a sharp intake of breath before he begins to make notes in a leather journal as he steps over congealing blood setting beside two SS corpses.

'Where's Capa when you need him, I could do with some good photographs of the scene.' He is muttering to himself; in a world of his own; in a world of words and detail and observation. He asks me to tell the story again and then fires questions at me with serious eyes that have lost their alcoholic sparkle. Questions followed by more questions.

'Where did Churchill sit?' he says, 'And the Colonel?' 'And they really drunk milk and laughed together?'

'Oui, monsieur.' He releases that booming laugh and slaps the jeep driver hard on the back who beams at him admiringly. When his pen finally stops he says to me:

'Join us, we will liberate Paris.'

'Monsieur, you do not have a gun. You cannot kill Nazis with ink.'

'There is much one can do with ink, Delphine. Do not mistake my lack of ammunition for passivity. Papa is a free soldier, baptised in the blood of the Spanish Civil War. A war correspondent is not permitted to carry a gun.' The jeep driver laughs as he pulls a Browning automatic from the depths of a canvas satchel slung loosely around his neck. I see the journal and a dog-eared map printed with the words *Fox Green.* His eyes follow mine.

'It's amazing what you can find washed up on a Normandy beach.' He tips his head back and drains a long slug from the silver hip flask.

'Papa,' I say, 'the Maquis have a plane hiding in the next town and there is underground press. We can print this Churchill story and drop it over Paris from the sky. The Parisians need to know that Churchill himself is here. It will give them courage.' As I motion a plane shape with my hands, I watch him ponder my suggestion and see a smile gradually form on his lips.

'Delphine, mon cherie, hop aboard and we will drink champagne in Paris. Vive la France!' He kisses me on both cheeks, grabs me with large arms and hugs me like a giant bear, and I feel the confident warmth of him and smell the alcohol that lines his breath. His enthusiasm is infectious and we liberate the next town with bullets and laughter and directions from a booming voice that has no rank but takes command with its reckless authority and precisely educated words.

While I recount my story of Winston Churchill to wide-eyed Maquis who gather at the underground press room beneath the bakery, Papa, who now seems to be a little drunk, types up the story on a typewriter he magics from nowhere. He refuses to use the one in the Press room, saying that he 'didn't bring this Baby halfway across the world to leave it sitting idle in the back of a jeep!'

When I return wet-eyed from the home of Frederick Saunier, Papa is bear hugging the petite Alfred who has printed the story on individual sheets and sent his son to deliver them to the plane. There were so many printed sheets, Alfred has run out of ink and they are taken by horse and cart to the plane that sits waiting in Longues field, five miles north of here. I leave the town happy, intoxicated by the sense of oncoming victory that I see in every eye that I look in. Saunier and many others died for this day.

We enter Paris atop a tank, with Papa sitting on the turret shouting orders in his loud voice. We are thirty strong and a mix of Papa's 4th Infantry and partisans from the surrounding countryside, who hold an assortment of weapons from pitchforks to Thompson submachine guns. Emotions are high and it is difficult to stop the killing as angry caged animals now run free and blood from our oppressors trickles in the gutter. And champagne corks pop as do bullets as the final snipers are shot and the Nazi regime is dismantled and collaborators executed quickly; without mercy.

Papa is good to his word and he drags me tipsily around the Place Vendome and introduces me to a deliriously happy Claude, the owner of the 'greatest establishment in Paris.' And we sit at a small, round table outside the Ritz with a bottle of *Cheval Blanc* and two glasses and smell the victory around us. Victory smells of burning metal and black smoke.

I could barely hear the oncoming plane above the revelry, such was the noise in the freed Paris streets. When the paper sheets started to rain down, I watched the multitude of faces gaze up and children's hands jump for them with gleeful smiles. I saw the freedom in their playful stance, limbs unsupressed, voices unchained and remembered what Saunier always said:

'For freedom, Christ set us free, so cast off your yoke of slavery.' I say it aloud and Papa eyes me seriously through champagne bubbles.

'Galatians 5, verse 1,' he says. And I am surprised that this brash American might know anything of God.

'I only ask to be free. The butterflies are free,' he says, 'Charles Dickens.'

And I watch this man through eyes filtered by champagne and wonder who he really is and as I ponder, lightheaded from alcohol and days without sleep, I watch a sheet of paper float towards us and land face up on the table. I am surprised at the sparsity of words in ink before me.

ERNEST HEMINGWAY LIBERATES PARIS!

Papa lets out a booming laugh.

Francis James Glib

The champagne bubbles had gone to my head and I felt giddy as I waited nervously in the small adjoining room. Develaire said he would send for me after he addressed the syndicate.

The small room I waited in had no windows and the lights were dim. I sat in an expensive brown leather sofa warming my hands by the flames of a roaring fire. One sensed that many animals died creating this seat, so guests could wait in comfort before being summoned. I could hear snatches of conversation above the crackling of wood. The orange embers drew my eyes in, away from a scattering of pine cones that rested in the hearth. The flames were bright and tall; the heat was oppressive and I felt an urge to remove my tie, but what would the syndicate think? I just placed a finger between neck and shirt to claim some temporary relief. I felt a sudden urge for water, a deep thirst. It surprised me because you forget the simple things when life is swimming in champagne and you hop from one engagement to another.

The flames lit up the bookcase in the alcove and I wandered over and absently ran a finger over some of the titles; *Mein Kampf*, Darwin's *Origin of Species*, Marx: *The Communist Manifesto. The Final Solution,* a book written by some long-forgotten Nazi General. I pulled it from the shelf, out of curiosity really, the gold emblazoned swastika catching the flickering half-light in contrast to the deep red cover. When I opened it, it was hand signed by Eichmann with a smudged date. Feb 1949?

An unusual collection. But I was not surprised, Develaire was an odd man despite his charismatic media persona. Glossy and smartly dressed, his surface finish shined brightly. I could hear his deep musical voice now as he addressed the syndicate. If I wasn't lazy I could have a chance of making this without him, without his money or influence. A moment of weakness and you are shaking hands with him on camera with an oily grin which becomes difficult to wash off. He is like a drug that captures you with its false euphoria and deceptive allure. When you discover his words are lies it is too late, the claws are deep and secure in your flesh, and to run away would be to lose everything. I am not prepared to lose everything, so I run with the money and the falseness, and drink champagne to hide from my conscience.

When I moved closer to the door the muffled voices in Develaire's private boardroom began to filter through.

'*Did you really need to kill the Deputy Prime Minister?*' A voice said sharply.

'*You are not linked to it, Hann, any messiness has been avoided.*' Develaire replied.

'*Yes, you always come out clean, but was it really necessary to kill him? And Caplin! The whole bloody country loved him!*'

'*Couldn't we have just bought him off like the rest?*' A different voice; I recognised the tone but couldn't bring her face to mind.

'*I didn't sign up for this. Too much uncertainty could ruin this country.*'

'*Settle down. Settle down.*' Develaire interceded. '*These men put their own principles before our great nation. It was a necessity to dispose of them. You are fortunate that I have covered our tracks and cleaned up the mess that you do not have the stomach to make.*'

'*But . . .*'

'*Enough! It is done. The bodies are buried and the way is paved for Glib to take over.*'

'*Are you sure of him? Are you sure he has what it takes?*'

'*He doesn't need to have what it takes, I do.*'

There was silence and I realised that any doubts from the syndicate were gradually being crushed. I could feel the sweat on my forehead and I felt a dull anger at the words uttered by Develaire. I would make a good Prime Minister, wouldn't I? I looked like a Prime Minister. I had principles but not too many. I had connections and influence inside this boardroom if nowhere else. I would . . . I could be good. The depressingly vocal doubt in me continued until I forced myself further from the door. I mean, how much of this does one want to hear.

'*Glib looks tidy and is starting to sound right, but he needs more work.*'

'*Glib will be fine.*'

'*Glib is our man and he understands the necessity of a harmonious relationship with the media . . . with us.*'

And then: '*And what of the Fox Club?*' And the murmurings and mutterings continued as many voices spoke loudly at once, until:

'*Quiet! The Fox Club doesn't exist.*' For the first time I heard a trace of doubt in Develaire's voice. He stumbled ever so slightly on the F in Fox. Maybe no one else heard it because they quickly started talking about money and shares, but it was there none-the-less. Had I not drunk so much champagne I would have remembered it the next day.

I sat back in the chair by the fire, feeling uncomfortable; it had nothing to do with the stifling heat.

When I was finally summoned it was by an overly tall man sporting a black turtle neck, who stooped to prevent his head knocking into the doorframe. His arms were long and lacked usual spontaneous movement as he looked through me with cold expressionless eyes.

'Are they r . . . ready for me?' I stammered, but he just held the door open with a slight inclination of his head, indicating I was to go through. A faint smoky odour lingered as I walked beneath his long extended arm. As I stood in the shadows in my bright blue jacket, my eyes surveyed the long oval table where twelve men in dark suits heatedly discussed a multitude of topics. When the thirteenth man arose in white tuxedo and pale skin, he looked like ice; his eyes sparkled like diamonds. And when Develaire clapped his hands together all voices were silenced as he said: '*Dear friends*, may I present to you, the future Prime Minister, Francis James Glib.'

As I shuffled from the shadows, I stepped into my unofficial inauguration. All eyes were upon me, waiting for words; words of inspiration, words of a leader. But all I could hear above the silent anticipation was the whisper inside my conscience. *What does it profit a man to sell his soul to gain the whole world?*

Spitfires Heading East

The mast of the wooden sailing boat that gradually rolled up on shore was broken in two. Wooden splinters pointed sharp and sodden up at the blue sky. A blue sky which appeared as suddenly as the storm had approached. The dark clouds drifted in wisps until the sun shone through, gently warming the unconscious man who lay drenched at the bottom of the boat, his bloodied head bandaged carefully with a yellow silk scarf. The charred Irvin jacket, laced with a faint aroma of cologne and pipe smoke, sat tight against his body.

***

Flight Lieutenant Tillard rested in a deck chair on the grass outside the hangar, watching flight sergeants repairing Chalky's Merlin engine. A couple of machine gun bullets brought it down late yesterday evening. Chalky almost bailed out amongst thick black smoke and enemy tracers, but he sat opposite Tillard now with a bottle of scotch between his knees, pretending to be asleep. Tillard knew he didn't sleep. Sleep brought on fear. Not a fear of death. Death he could greet happily knowing he had lived a life, however brief. His fear was incineration; burning alive in the cockpit of his Spit'.

The fox terrier, Skip, barked as the siren sounded and 'sleeping' pilots grabbed helmets, and cast away novels and cards, exchanging them for goggles and parachutes. Tillard winked at Chalky, who joked with the mechanics and boarded his fighter with ease. Propellers turned. Chalky motioned with fingers tugging at his collar, jesting at Tillard's chunky roll neck sweater, inappropriate for this hot August weather. But it was lucky; he daren't take it off, he'd worn it since day one and he'd never been hit.

The radio crackled with static: 'Stokers over the Isle of Wight, patrol head east'.

'The sun's behind us,' Tillard shouted with thumbs up.

'Good fortune, Tilly old boy,' Chalky shouted back.

At twenty-one, Tillard was the grandad of the group, since Squadron Leader Weston got shot down last week over the Channel. He drowned in the sea. His body washed up on Alverstoke Bay, blackened and barely recognisable by his poor mother. The funeral was in Scotland. Tillard represented the squadron, standing by her, digesting his own grief clouded with memories of the charred corpse. Weston's gold band was a family heirloom, she said. With tear-filled eyes she placed the ring in his large, shaking palm, closing his fingers around it. There were no heirs now – her beautiful boys were dead. The ring was small, almost too small to fit his large fingers.

Chalky couldn't talk about the death of Weston. Couldn't even attend the funeral. The chaps loved the Squadron Leader. Tillard took Skip; that dog was devoted to Weston, ever since he rescued it from mud banks near Portsmouth. Foolish thing to do, but Weston took chances, except in the air. In the air he was a master; a bird shot down before all feathers had grown.

The patrol flew in a classic V shape, with Tillard taking point. The Spitfire had been a joy to fly even when exhausted; he used to feel euphoric every time he left the runway. The only thing that gave him satisfaction was killing krauts. Anonymous faces descending to their death in smoky spirals. He hated them with a vengeance and notched up the most hits in the sqaudron; even more than poor old Weston, who was a far better pilot. Coburn said it was because Tillard flew with anger. Tillard laughed off the comment but knew it was true. The anger ate at him, polluting the joy of flight. Every time he thought of his father the memory of glinting eyes and wide, open smile was quickly replaced by thoughts of the bomb that destroyed the southern warehouses of the dockyard. There were no bodies to bury, only discarded limbs. They couldn't even find his watch; a beautiful timepiece passed down by his grandfather.

Curved Spitfire wings cut through sparse cloud and Tillard began to feel hot under the tight weave of the white sweater. He stopped himself from daydreaming when he saw the intensity of the storm in the distance. It was far off but seemed to approach with an uncanny speed threatening to overtake them. Enemy fighters! A legion of black dots suddenly broke free from the swirling mass of clouds. The cunning and audacity surprised Tillard. For a moment he admired his foe.

'Bandits!' whispered Coburn over the radio. You could hear the shock in his voice.

'Stay focussed chaps. No mercy.' *No mercy,* Tillard thought angrily. Happy-go-lucky Weston just shouted *Tally Ho!* Very British, and they all loved him for it. Loved him for his confidence, his skill and easy, care-free manner. Tillard they respected. But his anger often spilled out in the wrong directions – after drinking rum in *The Wheatsheaf,* occasionally in the mess if they left the fat on his bacon. Once he kicked Weston's dog.

By the time they reached the Channel the storm spat its contents out with ferocity; five Messerschmitt 109s and two Heinkels at 6000ft, itching to take on the remnants of 257 Squadron. There could be no element of surprise so Tillard peeled off with Heeley to his right and was above the far enemy fighter before it could react. A spray of bullets. Tillard smiled through gritted teeth. Smoke poured out of its dying carcass as it span out of control, exploding before it hit the sea. But Tillard spent too long watching his victory and a Heinkel stealthily approached, peppering his fuselage before he could manoeuvre into a sharp dive to throw off pursuit.

'Yellow 1. Yellow 1, bandit on your tail.' Tillard pulled out of the dive too late as a skilful Messerschmitt finished off what the Heinkel had started, blowing off his tail and sending him in an uncontrollable spiral. Lightning struck him as he went down, and all he could think was, 'This is it' as the darkness of the clouds swirled around him and the lightning lit up the sky – shocking him with the black silhouette of the Heinkel's pilot as the German warbird turned, searching for more prey. He blacked out for what seemed like a moment, but as he drifted in and out of consciousness broken words crackled in the air. Disjointed phrases yet somehow connected – they were the same voice. You can't burn me, Tillard thought. He would say this over and over to the unconscious voice in his head. And the lightning struck him again and again. And it hurt, leaving flashes in his mind; pictures of himself as a young boy running through fields with his brother, chasing an old, three-legged fox. Flash! Another, of an old man with a walking stick being introduced on stage as one of *The Few*. 'Squadron Leader ...'. Tillard doesn't hear his name, he just watches the man nervously finger the ring on his little finger.

A final bright flash then blackness. All is quiet and Tillard's mouth whispers words through almost soundless lips, 'Someone will remember us, even in another time.'

***

'Mayday, mayday. Maifeiertag, Maifeiertag!'
'Man overboard! *Hilfe!*'
'Sailor stranded in high seas. *Hilfe*. Help!'
'Stranded.'

'Hans!' the sailor screamed again as he watched his brother pulled away and under by the terrifying power of the waves. Ten foot breakers lurched the boat and as the lightning flashed a second time it struck the radio. It sizzled, crackled and died. Lightning struck the mast, cracking it in two. It plunged downward, knocking his head. Blood poured freely and he crumpled to the deck.

When he came to, the metallic taste of blood mingled with the salt on his lips. Above the howling wind he could hear a shout; the waves had lessened but were still fierce. The shout was faint against the loudness of the storm and groggily he stood up only to be knocked off his feet again. The second attempt was successful and he was greeted by the sight of a man in flying goggles and a yellow scarf desperately clasping onto a floating plane wing.

'Help!' the man's voice drifted towards him. The pole that reached him was held by the German sailor who was terrifying to behold, with blood running from his rain splattered head into his eyes.

Tillard grabbed the pole with one hand and the side of the boat with the other as it tossed ferociously. He could barely hold on until the firm clasp of the sailor yanked him to relative safety.

'Thank you!' he shouted, exhausted but gratefully into the wind.

'My brother! Have you seen my brother?' the sailor screamed at him. His face was contorted. He shouted over the side of the boat in guttural tones: 'Kleiner bruder! Where are you?'

The German words were an unconscious trigger. Quickly, Tillard unholstered his side arm and fired. Nothing happened as the wet pistol misfired; he threw it at the sailor then charged. They landed in a pile of fists as the angry waves continued to toss the boat precariously and Tillard pinned him down with his knees and put his hands around his throat, squeezing maniacally.

'Nazi scum!'

Tillard looked down into the sailor's blue eyes, the redness of the man's lips, the shape of his nose. A cross sat on a chain around the man's neck next to his hands. *His hands.* He loosened them slightly, the man coughed. He had killed many Germans, faceless black silhouettes flying enemy fighters. This was different, this was hands and skin and breath. He removed his fingers and began to move away. The sailor was sobbing, his body racked with exhaustion and grief.

'My brother, my brother, the sea has taken him.' Tillard watches him sob and shake as the blood from a gash on his head continues to run down his face. He unconsciously removes the silk scarf and wraps it carefully around the sailor's head. The sailor's body shakes uncontrollably and Tillard removes his Irvin jacket, wraps it around him tightly and holds him close with the remaining warmth of his body.

The ferocity of the storm gradually abated as the beginnings of stars twinkled in the night sky. The boat now bobbed gently as the two men propped each other up in the hull. Tillard was burnt and now that the adrenaline had disappeared it stung excruciatingly.

'Why did you rescue me?' he whispers to the sailor.

'You look like my brother; like me.'

And all the anger inside him dissolved with the final gusts of the storm and he sobbed into the sailor's shoulder.

The mast of the wooden sailing boat that gradually rolled up on shore was broken in two. Wooden splinters pointed sharp and sodden up at the blue sky. A blue sky which appeared as suddenly as the storm had approached. The dark clouds drifted in wisps until the sun shone through, gently warming the unconscious man who lay drenched at the bottom of the boat, his bloodied head bandaged carefully with a yellow silk scarf. The charred Irvin jacket, laced with a faint aroma of cologne and pipe smoke, sat tight against his body.

It was a combination of the sun and the dull repeated knocking of the hull on the rocky shore-line that woke the sailor. His head was sore and his legs unsteady as he jumped out onto the sandy beach. There was no one in sight, just seagulls and clear blue sky. Looking back he could see the pistol lying in the bottom of the boat. He remembered the hands that pulled the trigger; the hands that held him as he shivered in the night.

He noticed the flag fluttering high in the breeze before he saw the crowd beneath it. He could hear the fabric ripple, he could see the fraying edges, touched by countless winds. An old man with a walking stick and medals addressed the crowd in a cracked voice, broken with time.

'... I should have died the night of the storm. Inside I was dying every night. Anger does that to you, it burns you inside.' He held up his burnt hands. 'I nearly killed a man with these hands. But his hands pulled me into the boat. An action that taught me to forgive; to let go. I fought alongside many brave men during the Battle of Britain, only one saved my life.'

The German sailor removed the Irvin jacket and watched Squadron Leader Tillard limp off stage as the crowd put their hands together.

The Death of Edward Pritchard

꙳

The funeral was small when my grandfather died. I was surprised because my father said he served with Churchill closely after the war. He even married Churchill's distant cousin, Edith, my grandmother. There's a black and white photo of the Prime Minister and my grandfather smoking cigars, laughing.

The day he was buried, autumn appeared with gold leaf and a slight chill beneath a sun sitting low in the sky. Around the grave, alongside green grass and freshly dug earth, a handful of black-suited mourners paid their respects. I watched them all and shook their hands and exchanged tight, solemn smiles. An old man in a trilby and herringbone jacket shuffled forward and placed a book on the coffin. It was orange and faded, with silver writing on the spine. My eyes gazed at it briefly and moved from the orange cover to the smiling face of the man who placed it.

'It's a first edition,' he says in an accent thick with European influence. Was it French underlined with hints of German? 'Shame the dust jacket is missing,' he adds.

'Have you read it?' I say, not entirely sure of the most appropriate question.

'Twice.' He holds out his hand, which carries a long scar that runs the entire length of his thumb down to his wrist. 'Albert Klein.' He says by way of introduction.

'What is the book?' I say to him, intrigued by the mystery.

'*The Storm on the Sea of Galilee,*' he says with a sudden sparkle to the eye. 'It's a comprehensive research into the journey of Rembrandt's painting of the same name.'

'Journey?' I say.

'*The Storm on the Sea of Galilee* has a long and interesting history. The painting has been stolen many times; it has seen many hands. The book is factually incorrect in places but it doesn't detract from the prose.'

'Oh.' I look at the book again, not sure what to say next.

'How did you know my grandfather?'

'I served with him during the war. The Colonel loved art.'

'The Colonel?'

Before I could ask him anything further he had turned away and started limping across the grass, weaving respectfully between gravestones. I thought about what he had said; I thought about how little I actually knew about my grandfather. There was always an air of secrecy surrounding him. I knew he had been close to Churchill, of which I had been immensely proud, but when I asked questions about what he did during WW2, my father had clammed up. I always found this odd because he loved history.

That day I never did find out who wrote the orange book. I watched the gravediggers cover it with damp soil. I chuckled as I conjured the comical image of my grandfather sitting in heaven, reading it with a smile on his face. He always read with a smile; I remember the upturned edges of his mouth. I remember sitting on his lap and watching his wrinkled face as he read *Emil and the Detectives*. I sometimes thought he read it for himself, not me. I wondered whether there would be a library in heaven. Surely there would be. It's quiet in heaven, isn't it?

I continued with the busyness of life and forgot about the orange book and the man with a limp, until I began to sort through boxes of grandfather's effects. My father gave me seven boxes.

'That is his entire stamp collection,' he said. 'Grandma thought you would like it.'

Five of the boxes were heavy with loose stamps; colourful squares jumbled and unsorted. The other two were packed with albums, neat and perfect, displaying stamps from every country imaginable. I was surprised to find the photo of Churchill and my grandad smoking cigars, loose in the last book. It made me think again of the unknown past. The near past is often a mystery that seems to be just out of reach, so I researched Colonel Edward Pritchard, my grandfather, with an obsessive fervour which always ended in frustration. Every path led to nothing prior to March 1952. Even Albert Klein had evaporated like a ghost in the night. I just know he was a bookseller from Paris. There was no address; no record of his death.

I thought about the book that was buried with my grandfather. I thought about it a lot. *The Storm on the Sea of Galilee;* I knew it was a clue and on more obsessive days I imagined digging it up with that rusty blue-handled shovel that lies unused in the shed. Sometimes I would wake at night, drenched in sweat, dreaming of the orange book lying on my grandfather's chest. It would always end with the police hauling me away in handcuffs for desecrating the grave of an unknown soldier.

'It's my grandfather!' I would shout, but my voice was incomprehensible words and syllables uttered in a strange guttural tongue.

After finishing shifts at the prison I would visit the library. At first it was just Thursdays but eventually every day until I had frequented all the libraries and bookshops in London. The libraries held many books entitled *The Storm on the Sea of Galilee,* but none with an orange cover. I read them all. In these books I learnt that *The Storm* was a priceless piece of art painted by Rembrandt van Rijn in 1633. From the photographs I could see it was a beautifully detailed painting. I would love to have seen it in a museum, but Klein had been right, it had been stolen a lot. It was last seen in Boston in 1992.

The day I found the orange book the sunlight shone through my window with a beautiful intensity. The quality of the air was still and I watched the light catch dust particles gently floating. Sometimes you only find what you are looking for when you stop searching. The day I gave up, I found the book sitting non-descript on a metal shelf, its orange edges fraying and scuffed with time. I looked at it with a mixture of disbelief and longing. The prisoner who owned it could see my desire for it and I swapped it for my watch and the £43.20 that remained in my wallet.

The book's contents were musty and brown. I found my grandfather dressed in German uniform on page 67 in a grainy photo with the caption, *Colonel von Zweifel's Ghost Patrol.* The dishevelled officer looking back at me was surrounded by six battle-weary men. His hands rested on the large walnut frame of *The Storm on the Sea of Galilee.*

Winston Churchill

— ⊶⊷ —

Dear Clementine, once again the black dog is chasing me. It descends on me shapeless and ugly and flat. It howls menacingly as I hide in the dark place beneath these rough, woollen sheets, devoid of hope, all accomplishments lost in the shadows of this alternate reality. Please be there when I return.

Days later when clarity returns, I peak above the cotton sheets and wonder at the sunlight resting on the net curtain. It seeps into the fabric bringing it to life. The water in the glass next to the bed remains cool and I enjoy the freshness. Yesterday the taste was dull like drinking from a puddle walked through by a thousand hedgehogs with dirty feet. Now it is crisp and clear.

My instinct is to read. It's what I always do after an episode. Words pull me back into reality, even fictitious ones, so I search for Conan Doyle in the drawers by the bed. Sherlock is nowhere to be seen. Clementine's had a clear out. There is nothing accept medicines and ironed handkerchiefs embroidered with the letter 'W'; and a small black Bible. Memories flood in at the touch. I finger the book's decaying edges; run my finger over the fading gold leaf writing. A hole, round and perfect, obliterates the letter 'L'. I trace the missing letter and think on this miracle as I turn the yellowed pages, musty with time. Reaching the page where the bullet ceased flight I read the passage aloud.

'Wir nehmen jeden gedenhen gefangen.' The guttural words taste rusty on my tongue. *We take every thought captive.*

Von Zweifel gave this to me the second time I met him, which was behind bars in a small Polish town bordering Germany. I forget its name. I do remember the date, Christmas Eve 1945. It was those first months after the war. The start of bleak years of repair and taking stock of what wasn't broken. Blackwood was my driver then; more than that, part of my inner circle. It's good to have a working man next to you, it keeps you grounded.

As I close the Book I remember von Zweifel, the Colonel without a hat. Before he gave me the Bible, he sent me a letter. The big Colonel with the hearty laugh was the last person I expected to hear from, but when I did I could tell he wasn't laughing any more. In his words I saw his own black dog chasing him down. A dog that snarled and bit and choked the life from him. His words were this:

Dear Mr. Churchill,
I doubt this letter will ever reach you, but there is no one else. No one can help. I have nobody, just my thoughts, black as they are. And time; too much of it. Sitting in this cell, it moves so slowly.
Do you remember me? Do you remember how we laughed around the farmhouse table? It seems an age ago. Was it really only last year? What a short space of time for a world to change. When I left you that day I walked out that door released from burdens. I recall how the wind touched my face. Freedom has a taste. I don't need to tell you that.
Mr. Churchill, I am not a bad man. A soldier has to kill, doesn't he? I was a good soldier; I did my duty. I was in possession of priceless art, stolen for the Führer, when they apprehended me. I was returning it to the monastery . . . but the detail doesn't matter, I only know that I have sat in this cell long enough. I know that the light that reaches my cell is dull and thin, and the darkness that fills every available space has started to consume me. Darkness so thick that I cannot move. It attacks me in waves and all I have is this rough grey blanket to hide inside and escape the rats that slowly devour my soul. The strength I once had has evaporated. How will I ever find Hannelore and Peter? It is clear that there are some battles men cannot fight; it would have been easier to have been shot against a wall.
Please release me.

Von Zweifel (Colonel)

My regret is that I didn't act straight away. I knew the black dog was chasing him . . . I could sense it in his words, but the busyness of office took me away. There are not enough hours.

Then one day Blackwood arrived earlier than usual and found me nattering with the cook, drinking a glass of milk.

'Do you remember the milk we drank in Normandy, sir? He said with a smile. I thought about the creamy milk and the Colonel laughing. I thought of his resolute face as he shot the two SS officers.

'Von Zweifel,' I say, and Blackwood nods knowingly.

Later, whilst Blackwood was packing, Clementine said, 'Why do you have to go to Poland now?' But I did. Because of the letter. Because of human duty. Because his words called to me, their tone urgent. Blackwood understood and drove us to the airport, commandeering a plane.

When Blackwood and I arrived in Poland it was beginning to snow and I was wrapped in the black greatcoat that served me well in the war. We reached the prison late at night, to find von Zweifel singing. A melody that I still do not know the name of but whistle often. His demeanour surprised me; I half expected him to be dead.

'Mr. Churchill!' he exclaimed, beaming. He looked terrible; grey skin and sunken cheeks; but his eyes were alive. I was surprised by the relief I felt.

'Your letter was a touch morose. I thought you might be dead,' I said wondering whether it had been foolish to come at all. I was not prone to unquantified impulse.

'Take every thought captive,' he said and placed the bullet holed Bible in my hand. One of the guards had taken pity on him and read to him every night.

'The guard said it saved his life,' he said, touching the black cover, 'it was in his pocket the day he got shot.' Zweifel recounted the story as if it were his own. I was sceptical, although I had seen many miracles. How else did we win the war if God was not with us?

Blackwood and I released the Colonel the same day. To my surprise, Blackwood tried to return him his luger. But he wouldn't take it.

Christmas Day we spent in a partially bombed hotel just inside Germany, eating what could have been chicken, accompanied by potatoes in their skins. There was no milk to be found anywhere but the whisky in Blackwood's kitbag fuelled laughter and warmed the soul. And we talked about Latin and art, which Zweifel seemed to be particularly knowledgeable of.

The destruction of Germany would make any man sad. Humanity has many faces. Sadder still was the brokenness I witnessed watching Zweifel kneel beside two graves. Mother and son. After this the light in his eyes seemed to be almost extinguished. He wanted to search for his daughter, Hannelore, but he was crushed and weak and I eventually persuaded him to return to England with me. In the years to come, Blackwood searched Germany and the rest of Europe but never found her. Not a trace.

Like Blackwood, von Zweifel was a useful man to have close. He fitted into my unofficial cabinet with ease as he gradually recovered from the trauma. He understood people and politics; he was gifted at reading body language and his English was almost perfect.

Although the country was recovering, these were difficult times with political unrest still abound. It troubled von Zweifel greatly. He said Britain was the anchor of Europe; Britain didn't have time for instability. He was worried. I didn't see him for days until he woke me late one night saying he had written out a protocol to keep this country safe, keep me safe. I read it over, twice. The words were inspired and creative, just like the plans for a bunker he had sketched out in grey pencil and shaded with care. There were copious notes in the margin.

'I should give them to the Prime Minister,' I said.

'You're the Prime Minister,' he said.

'Not anymore.'

'You will be again.'

That same week I introduced him to the architect, Hathaway.

'Edward Pritchard, meet Arthur Hathaway. You two are going to be great friends,' I said, and walked off to find Clementine so they could become acquainted. It was much later, after I found him dancing with my cousin Edith, that he said to me, 'Edward Pritchard?'

'That's your new name, Zweifel. The name of the President of the Fox Club.' The rest is history, the detail of which is buried beneath layers of secrecy.

Robert Capa

There were many interesting faces I photographed in Normandy as the conflict moved off the beaches at the back end of June. Two I remember distinctly. Their faces said everything but their mouths were silent. Maybe it's because they didn't speak that I remember them the most.

The last day of June 1944 was hot and dry like a sun-scorched desert. The line of prisoners was exhausted, with heads drooping from compounded fatigue. The 1st Infantry medic handed out water like the bargirl at Lou-Lou's. I felt parched myself. I had since D-Day. The day of days I was trying to forget. I risked my life for these photographs and some schmuck back in England over-developed them. But I'm not dead, which Papa said was a blessing, as he laughed and hugged me and raised his hip flask in mock salute. 'Were you really there?' he jibed as he wrote my latest *story* in short staccato sentences in his journal.

I'm snapping away carefully with my Contax now, wiping dust from the lens with a khaki sleeve, feeling blessed that my favourite camera remained free from seawater. I held it high that day when I returned to the boat, stray bullets zinging through the water, straps dangling above my head. I was soaked in water and blood but the Contax was dry. Thank God. I love this camera.

My lens captures fresh water spilling down the chin of a prisoner, his image catches my eye but the picture is nothing special. I can sense it. Sense whether the shot is good or bad, whether it has depth. The camera is part of me, like Papa and his pen. When I look around for a new target the picture before me is perfect and I see it with clarity before I have even taken the first shot. I move forward quickly. Click, click, click. I am real close and the steely-faced SS officer with a defiant far-off gaze ignores me while the MP searches him with uncaring hands. His meanness is palpable; deep-rooted, emerging from the depths of his smooth, youthful face. There's a knife in his long boot; it is curved and sheathed in black leather and matches his trench coat, which he holds open with expert hands. His mean eyes pierce through the policeman. Dark hair springs forth from a white bandage wrapped around his head, the tail end loose on his shoulder next to the twin lightning strikes of the SS lapel patch. Was he older than twenty? I doubt it. I offered him my canteen and then a smoke, so I could get the measure of him, but he refused both with a look of disdain from his eyes. He was processed and moved on quickly without a word from his lips. I could sense the policeman was wary of him. Like Papa, he was cautious of the SS.

'They don't care if they die. They have an appetite for pain,' Papa told me.

'I know,' I said, 'I see it in their eyes. The camera never lies,' I say. When you get close enough the truth of the person is clarity in black and white.

The German boy with hair the colour of straw reminded me of my brother. I don't know why. Maybe that was why I looked at him again. I watched him drawing circles in the sand with his finger. His sad eyes were intent on the sand before him so he didn't look up when I took the photograph. Despite being caged, the other boy soldiers were playing and laughing together, relaxed in the confidence that Americans don't shoot prisoners.

A flock of B52s flew overhead with noisy engines and all eyes were drawn to them as their large wings cast shadows on the beach. Except the boy, who continued to look down in the yellow sand, even when Corporal Jackson handed out Hershey bars to yelping soldiers who had begun to play like boys again. That second day I photographed the boys, Hitler's Youth, playing some rough football-type game with the sort of zeal that you feel when you know you are free. Which was ironic, because they were actually in a wired cage guarded loosely by military police. Several times the ball hit the straw haired boy, but he never looked around, just continued to make circles in the sand with his index finger.

When he saw me the 1st Infantry medic came over and asked me if the boy had moved since yesterday.

'Looks like he has been sitting there all night,' I say. 'Hey, kid, are you alright?' I shout. He doesn't look up. Nothing. The medic and I look at each other then we enter the cage. I snap the boy's photograph as he is led from the cage by the medic. I look through the lens. The haunting look I see would horrify me in one so young if I had not seen many times before in Spain. It's the last picture I take that day. I know its good; I feel it.

I return to the array of tents shared by photographers and correspondents and after wiring the roll back to *Life* magazine, I head off to my bunk only to find Papa asleep in it.

'Hey Papa!' I say, shaking him. 'Wake up its time for a game.'

And we play cards with Pyle and Vandivert, and pass whisky around till we are all a little tipsy, and the sad face of the straw-haired boy has been forgotten, now hidden behind three Jacks which I bet on with practised indifference. I rake in dollars and those fake invasion notes that we are starting to use for currency.

When I awake blurry-eyed, the boy with hair the colour of straw is in the tent doorway, looking at my camera.

'Hey, kid,' I say, but he doesn't look up. Maybe he is deaf. 'You assigned to me?' I say a little louder, joking. Nothing – he just stares at my camera. A thought occurs to me and I search through my knapsack and find the Leica I stole from the charred corpse lying next to a pill box on Omaha Beach. I hand it to the kid. His eyes are still expressionless but his dirty hands touch it delicately like he was scared it would break.

'You have it, kid,' I say, thinking that this would be the end of the matter, but he spends the day following me around, snapping mock pictures, using the Leica, copying my every stance or position. He doesn't smile or even appear to be enjoying himself, I just get a sense that he is at least partially happy as he mimics my every move.

'Who's the shadow?' Papa says to me when I return with the boy in tow. 'Your apprentice? I preferred that dog back in England!'

I laugh. 'He likes taking photos, Papa.' 'Ignore him,' I say, whispering to the boy, who doesn't acknowledge me but is looking at some photographs that Vandivert has processed in the dark tent down the 'alley'.

'At least put some film in it,' Papa says accusingly. Papa loves strays too.

'Sure I will, after lunch.'

After lunch I show the kid how to use the camera. He won't look me in the eye but he touches the Contax around my neck.

'No, no! Not this baby!' I say and he winces like I am going to hit him. 'Hey kid, sorry. Use the Leica – it is good German technology.' And he holds it in his hand in a certain instinctive way, the way I held a camera for the first time. The way I hold it every time.

That afternoon it was my turn to follow him and I take photos of him taking photos. He photographs the prisoners' football, the wheel of Papa's commandeered jeep, some coins left on the card table. He takes several of the clock in Ernie's tent and watches the second hand sweeping. He has no sense of time so I gently push him on. It's only later, when he photographs the circles he draws in the sand, I realise that every picture he has taken is of something round.

'What's with you and circles, kid?' I say amused.

When we return to the tent the 1st Infantry medic is there, saying there is space on a hospital ship back to London and it might be good for him to be on board. When he goes I load him with rolls for the Leica, which he grips hold of tightly, scared I am going to take it away.

'It was swell shooting the war with you, kid,' I say by way of goodbye. And although he is silent, his eyes look at me directly for the first time and I smile as he takes my picture.

'The picture never lies, kid. If your pictures aren't good enough, you're not close enough.'

Ten years later, in the May of 1954, I was marching with French infantry through the sodden soil of Indochina when I heard some of the guys talking of a British photographer with a German accent; he was making headlines photographing the moon using new technology. He called himself Endre.

I thought of the silent boy and his Leica as I trod through mud in army boots and khaki slacks. Gentle rain droplets fell into the puddles before me. I watched the circles expand across the dirty water, the distance ever increasing. It came to me clearly: we unconsciously touch people's lives in unknown ways; we change their direction by a word or an action. We send ripples that can change generations. I thought of this and many other things as I marched. And I prayed deep inside of me that I had led a good life.

Grey (Inspector) (2)

—e·o—

11.59am

Do you believe in coincidence? I don't.

It sounds cliché but the truth of the matter is that good policemen follow hunches. So when I walk into *The Cricketers* to contemplate the unusual events of the last couple of hours, the barman tells me the Guinness is off and pours me a pint of a guest ale from a barrel out back.

'What is it?' I say.

'A new Porter, *Black Rook*,' he says.

'What?'

'*Black Rook*. The name of the stout,' he says exasperated, like I haven't been listening properly.

Black Rook.

'Oh,' I say and my mind, which is beginning to become less foggy as the codeine kicks in, is connecting seemingly inconsequential events with natural born instinct.

'There's a micro-brewery down at the farm. Apparently Frank Caplin owns it . . .' 'Owned it,' the barman corrects, remembering that Caplin died this week.

As he witters on I'm not really listening, I'm looking at the thick blackness of the liquid before me and the condensation on the glass. It is only when he is silent that I realise I have placed the gun on the table with a heavy thud, brown wood absorbing the sound. I flash my badge to reassure the barman that I am still a policeman, drink the stout in one and ask him politely if I can borrow his vintage yellow Citroen.

'You will take care of it?' he says anxiously.

'Yes,' I lie, 'I'm a policeman.'

1.01pm

Within half an hour I'm parked on the large gravel driveway that is the entrance to Black Rook Farm, as a Rottweiler greets me with bared teeth. My pulse is quickened by adrenaline; I always feel like this when I know I am on the right track. But I feel on edge too, so I point the Browning at the dog. Surprisingly he backs off and I follow him through an arch of twisted wisteria, as he runs around the back of the large house, straight into the kitchen. There I am confronted by a man holding a pheasant in one hand and a shotgun in the other. The barrel is aimed at my chest.

'Who are you?' he says, irritated, 'I'm always happy to shoot intruders.'

'Inspector Grey,' I say and realise I am pointing the Browning at him. I place it slowly down onto a table by the door and carefully draw my badge from my jacket.

'I've told the police everything. Quit scaring my dog and get out.'

'I ... I don't know why I am here,' I say, which was the truth. Why am I here? He looks at me puzzled, frowning.

'I thought you had come to ask about Uncle Frank. I told the Chief Inspector he was murdered, but no one believes me.'

'Why do you think that?' I say.

'He was old, Inspector, but there was nothing wrong with his health. He didn't even need glasses. All his private healthcare records have disappeared so I can't prove anything.'

'Who would want him dead?' I say.

'Who knows ... ' He lowers the twin barrels of the shotgun and places it on a long farmhouse table alongside cup rings, scorch marks and solidified candle wax. On the table I see half eaten toast and the remains of coffee.

'People get uncomfortable with the truth, Inspector. There's no money in it,' he adds. I notice the dog follows him closely and continues to eye me with suspicion. He strokes it reassuringly, resting one hand against red bricks that surround an Aga.

I am not sure what to say or what to do, and I wish I hadn't drunk the wine and the stout because now my thinking is cloudy.

'Have you got any clues?' I pull weakly from nowhere.

'Clues?'

141

'Yes. Anything that may help catch. . . the murderer.' He looks at me and I can tell from his expression he is deciding whether I'm worth the time.

'Wait here,' he says, and disappears through a door that steps down into a hallway. When he returns he is holding a brown envelope, which he passes to me.

'I found this in my uncle's study.' In the envelope is a small silver key, etched B257, and a business card from a doctor at the university.

'Dr Edison, Senior Lecturer in Criminology and Psychology,' I read out loud. 'Do you know this guy?'

'I've never heard of him.'

I call the number on the card but the line is dead.

Before I leave with the key in one pocket and the gun in the other, Caplin's nephew says to me: 'Do you believe, Uncle Frank was murdered?'

'Yes.' I say, and I know it's the truth.

2.57pm

The path that leads to the Science Campus is lined with roughly sculpted hornbeams. I notice the greenness of their leaves and the tight cluster of the twisting branches. Had I lived a different life I would have designed a pathway like this; a beautiful long entrance lined with uniform green foliage. They would have led to antique steps guarded by lions, weathered by time and wind and snow.

The path leads to steps cluttered with students who peel away from me like age was contagious. I ask the woman at the Information Point for directions to Doctor Edison's office. Her blank expression is followed by five minutes of searching on databases and Google, and even some handwritten A4 book from 1996. The receptionist looks surprised when I show her the business card but she shrugs her shoulders nonetheless. There is nothing else to say. When I flash my badge she gives me directions to the staff room, which I quickly forget. By the time I have taken the second left, which is an endless corridor punctuated by rooms and posters, I am lost in the depths of academia.

I can't find the staff room, just a dead end filled with four rows of grey-green lockers of varying sizes. They are numbered randomly. I find B257 easily, slip the key in and wrestle with the warped door until it is prized open. I gaze at the *Ferris Bueller* poster hanging loosely with yellow faded tape, until my eyes fall upon a small file which rests at the bottom. I open it and flick through a document on Sir Anthony Develaire and circumstantial evidence linking him to a French assassin named Jean Argentan. There is also a hand-written file entitled *The Truth Behind the Marie Celeste*, out of which falls a hazy black and white image of a tall man wearing a wide-brimmed hat.

I ponder the stack of unanswered questions before me when I feel my phone vibrating beneath my jacket. There are twelve missed calls, all from the Chief. I don't want to phone him; I feel exhausted, despite the initial excitement of the leads. When I look at the screen the numbers start to blur in front of me and I search my pockets for the remaining codeine, only to find the cold metal of the Browning. Despite the boundaries I have crossed, duty still binds me to my uniform, so I return the Chief's call and hear expletives drowned out by the sounds of a slightly hostile crowd.

'Grey, where are you?'

'I'm following up some leads, sir.'

'I've been trying to call you. Haven't you been watching the news?' He's irritated.

'No sir.'

'The Prime Minister's addressed the nation about the recent deaths. Now there's an agitated crowd outside St David's.'

'Oh.'

'Oh! Get down here Grey, I need you. And take your phone off silent, dammit!'

4.11pm

Destiny is often played out in slow motion. The crowd is thick outside of St David's. It matches the atmosphere; it tastes of uncertainty like the potential threat of a firework prematurely extinguished. My eyes seem to have a hazy clarity to them as I search for a way through to the Chief, who stands close to the large oak doors of the church. I am familiar with Prime Ministerial security and the lack of tough, decisive men in black suits alarms me. I stand on the bonnet of the yellow Citroen to attain a better view, then the roof, as the barman's prize car gets swamped by a tide of humanity. There are two types of faces in the crowd; genuine protesters with handwritten boards and concern on their faces, and the paid trouble makers who are dotted everywhere. They are isolated spots of cancer; bad apples. Above mumbled chanting and the noise of dissatisfaction, there is the sound of breaking glass and I realise the weight of the crowd has pushed the rear screen in. I wipe sweat from my lip. I feel it run down my back. The crowd makes me nervous and I rest my hand on the reassurance of the gun.

When I see the Prime Minister walk through the doors I know he is an imposter; I know that he is a fake. He walks the same and his face seems identical at distance, but even though my eyes are struggling to focus, I am certain it is not the Prime Minister. I feel the certainty in my gut.

'That's not him,' I mouth. 'That's not the Prime Minister!' I shout. But no one hears me. I am invisible in this crowd; in every crowd. I am alone; isolated. Present but not part of it. Like every day at the station.

The gun is heavy and firm and reassuring. It feels good in my hand like it's supposed to be there. It fits perfectly, my fingers curled tightly around the handle, my index finger poised on the smooth curve of the trigger. Deep down I know that a gun separates. It separates life from death; it cuts a man from his soul. But I sense the power of the weapon; the hold it has on me; the hold it has had since loading the bullets into the chamber. With these last thoughts, I pull the trigger and become one with death. And although there is something very wrong in this, I forget why. And the threatening noise of the crowd is beautifully silenced in this single moment, as the imposter lies still in a pool of his own blood. For a handful of seconds I have control of the whole world.

11.59pm

Later I'm being questioned. The story of the fake Prime Minister doesn't wash with the Chief Inspector and to be honest, an hour later, even I don't believe it any more. Apparently there's a mixture of codeine and alcohol in my blood.

Snared Rabbit

———— ❦ ————

I send Henry and Stitch to check the snares for rabbits and push the red baseball cap further down on my head; the sun's in my eyes. I leave the other boys playing pirates on the beach. They run around whooping and shouting and splashing in the water, and I wonder how long I can keep them together. They were excited about rescuing the man in the car. I have long given up being surprised by what gets washed up on our beach. I told the boys the driver was sleeping, but he was clearly dead. I checked his pulse when I stole his watch. At least that was still ticking; looks old and military.

I never presumed that today would be so profitable but when I head up the steep, gritty pathway that leads off the beach, I find a ten pound note trapped in a prickly gorse bush. The early rising beachcombers and birders must have missed it, intent on different treasure.

Running close to the coastal path there are secluded dusty car parks near the cliff edge. I always check the bins up there for glass lemonade bottles manufactured by Partridges in town. It's habit really. They only give ten pence a bottle but find enough and you can buy a loaf of bread down at the bakery. Which is something when you are feeding twelve.

The third bottle I find today is cracked. I notice the black car when I throw the bottle from the cliff edge – hopeful it will hit the sea. Two men stand close to the edge looking out, their conversation just faint mutterings muffled by coastal wind. I am stealthy, so when I see the passenger side window open, I sneak up to it quietly and steal the black jacket on the seat. It smells of expensive cologne and smoke. The conversation floats towards me:

'Ignore what the news is reporting. The Prime Minister's not dead. Fontaine got him out. She's following protocol.'

'Fox Club protocol?'

'Yes, the bloody Fox Club protocol! Now use it. Get to the bunker and finish what we started.'

The conversation's tone is nasty. Unsettled by the voices I leave the scene and cycle to town on the rusty BMX Henry found in a skip last summer. I am wearing the stolen black jacket, which is making me hot, so I sell it to Nate down at the market. He checks it over with a keen eye. 'Expensive threads, man. How much you want for it?'

'Tenner?' I say and he gives me the money quickly so I know I've sold it cheap, but business is business, as long as everyone gets their cut. I turn to go but he calls me back.

'Do you want this?' he says, and holds out a small memory card, 'It was in the jacket pocket.'

I look at it closely between thumb and forefinger then slip it into my rucksack, because one thing I have learnt is that everything has value. You can sell anything.

Away from the market square narrow cobbled lanes lead to cafes and windows selling ice creams of every flavour and colour. The ice cream tubs are like an artist's pallet and in my head I mix the green of pistachio with the pink of rhubarb. I see the colours merge. I walk past McQueen's bookshop and see the spines lined up through the window. I can't read the titles but I notice an image of *Tintin* etched in gold. When I go through the door opposite, Mr Winters the antiques dealer is pleased to see me.

'Hello, Captain,' he says, 'what you got for me today?'

I like Winters; he always offers me tea and a slice of lemon drizzle cake baked by his mother. He still lives with her; he's lonely, the poor guy. Sometimes on grey days I wish I had a mother who baked me drizzle cake.

'I found this,' I say, showing him the watch. It has a black face and fluorescent green hands. He holds it to his ear.

'Still ticking. Nice. It's a Waltham. World War Two issue. They don't make 'em anymore.'

'How much, Mr Winters?' I say.

'The market's not great at the moment. I can give you a score.'

We always play this game. It's just how it works. A 'score' means it's

146

probably worth one hundred, maybe two hundred pounds. So I haggle and he sighs often and pretends to be offended. It goes back and forth until I am sitting with seventy quid in my back pocket and a strong cup of tea in my hand. I am drinking out of cracked Clarice Cliff china which he says is too far gone to sell. I like the china; the oranges and blacks and yellows; the patterns. All her china has style. I can say that because when I am not selling, I am an artist. I notice things. Colours, patterns, detail.

I now have ninety pounds in my pocket and I'm full from tea and the large chunk of drizzle cake, so I stop thinking about food, and wonder whether I should treat myself and buy some new pencils and paper from Tally's art shop. It's on the corner by the square next to the water fountain. I love drawing and painting.

I sold a painting once. I took a day off and sat in the square and painted the bright market stalls and bustling people. A man with a dog collar and brown leather jacket stood over me. He watched me paint and asks if I want to sell it.

'It's a hundred pound,' I said, 'and I'll sign it when I am finished.' I was joking but he stood there thoughtful for a moment then said:

'OK. Come down to the church and I will find some money.'

I took a blade because I feel suspicious; there was no haggling; it was too easy. The church was just a building like any other; it was nothing special. Inside was the same; nothing ornate or gold or showy.

'Where's your pews and altar and stained glass,' I said to him almost accusingly.

'We haven't got any,' he said.

'How would God know to visit here on Sundays?'

'God is not in things or rituals,' he said, 'they are empty and meaningless. God is with us every day. Don't you see him in the sun and the grass and feel Him in the wind? Don't you see Him in your friends' faces?'

I left that day with two fifty pound notes. He made me think, so next Sunday I brought all the boys. They sat at the back, fidgeting and whispering until I tell 'em to be quiet. My painting was hung on a plain cream wall, a riot of colours disrupting the calm sanctuary. I watched a man get baptised. He talks about freedom through Jesus but I don't really hear his words, I don't need to, I see it in his face.

We sleep in the dilapidated warehouse on Hankey's Farm. You have to walk through three fields to get to it. It's right down the end of a long, dusty track. It is made of wood that is dry and old and decaying. The corrugated iron roof is rusty in places but it keeps us dry. We always repair the roof because you may as well live outside if you're going t' get wet. It used to hold a large printing press, so the space isn't that cosy, but we've made it our own. It's bloody freezing in the winter when the firewood's run out.

Sometimes we work for Old Man Hankey. He's mean so he likes free labour. On those days we work hard and long and he turns a blind eye to us boys staying on his property. He says the old warehouse was his uncle's before he died of chicken pox in '84.

'You don't die from chicken pox,' I say.

'Complications,' he says, ''twas the pox I tell yer. The warehouse is mine by inheritance, you boys need to work for me twice a week.' And I shake on it, not because I'm afraid or intimidated by him, despite his shotgun, but 'cos I can tell he is sad and alone, even though he has a house and farm and tractor.

'You don't need things, you need people,' I said to him one time and I was surprised by the wisdom in it. But he pretends like he isn't listening.

When I open the warehouse door I feel guilty about the pencils and paper hidden from view inside the rucksack. Several pairs of small feet run over.

'Hey, Captain! What you got?' And there's four sets of hands patting my rucksack.

'Careful, careful,' I say. And I dish out chocolate bars and apples to eager hands. 'Eat the apples first.' They all groan but do as I say. I'm the Captain, aren't I.

Sully is gently boiling dinner over an open fire. The smell is pleasant and wafts over to me with the scent of pepper as he smiles, looking for my approval.

'How's dinner going, Sully?' I say, looking into the browning soup-like mixture.

'Fine, Cap', plenty of vegetables.'
'Rabbit stew?' I say hopefully.
'Yeah, without the rabbit.'
'Henry and Stitch not back yet?'
'Nah.'

My bedroom is the old foreman's office with a large desk and shelves. It's the only separate room in the whole warehouse. When the door's closed the boys don't come in; they know I'm painting. They like it when it's open. There is a stack of Beatrix Potter books on the desk. I copy the pictures with water colours and hang them on a string line that circles the room. There's loads of them because my paintbrush is fast and accurate. At night I look at them by candlelight and wonder how I can do this; where this gift came from.

Sometimes I get angry. The little boys ask me to read and I can't do it. I see in pictures and colours; the writing is just black and stiff and frustrates me. I have a friend at the village bakery that is helping me to read. Stacey. She is an unusual character but her heart is big, like the man from the church.

'Why do you want to read Beatrix Potter?' she says, 'the words are so difficult.' And she's right, I have never heard of *soporific* or *alacrity*. But we read them anyway.

Stacey owns the bakery in the village but she doesn't work there; she works in the cellar beneath, with her son Alfie, who is twelve like me. She has a computer and I know she uses these memory cards like the one from the suit pocket. So I head off to the bakery, knowing that she will give me some money for it because today has been lucky and it is not over yet.

The bakery always smells amazing. You can smell it before you even reach Orchard Lane. Apart from the Post Office it's the only shop in the village; there's not even a pub. The boys love donuts but I buy fresh crusty bread; if Henry and Stitch don't come back with the rabbits the boys will need filling up.

Down in the cellar Stacey and Alfie work on multiple laptops. There's wires and leads and all sorts of machinery that come from a world I no longer live in.

'Hey Captain, what brings you here?' Stacey says when I walk down the steps.

'Hey Stace, do you wanna buy this?' And I hold out the memory card between thumb and forefinger.

'Yeah, sure. Where did you get it?'

'A suit jacket,' I say. Stacey doesn't care that I'm a thief. She's a thief too. She steals information that's not hers and sends it out across the internet. She has an online magazine called *The Liberator*. Most of the media is just lies, she says, and it's her duty to make sure people hear the truth.

'Who gave you this?' she says to me urgently.

'I stole it.'

'Captain, this is massive.' And she turns the screen so I can watch the video playing. On it I see the two men that were talking by the cliff edge. What they say doesn't mean much to me so I look at Stacey, puzzled.

'That's Anthony Develaire,' she says pointing to one of the figures on the screen, 'this conversation connects him to the death of the Deputy Prime Minister.'

I've never seen her so animated. She gives me twenty quid and hugs me. When I leave I hear her tell Alfie to send it out to the web. I can hear the excitement in her voice – it's contagious.

I catch up with Henry and Stitch by the time I get to the dip in the second field. The shadows are long. The boys walk slowly in a kind of zigzag pattern like they have all the time in the world. I heard them laughing a quarter of a mile away. They hold up the rabbits in victory when they see me coming.

'We got 'em Captain!' they shout.

'Well done lads. I knew you would.'

When you're hungry, nothing tastes better than snared rabbit.

Amelia (2)

—⌒⌒—

'Without a sword in his hand he struck down the Philistine and killed him.' **1 Samuel 17: 50**

***

There's no air under the blanket. All is still and in this moment I stop time.

Poddy Flower is snoring. He is under the blanket so I wake him with a pat on the back. I hold his long ears with both hands and look into his big, brown eyes. Daddy says they are the colour of conkers.

What's all the noise?

'I don't know,' I whisper to Poddy, but I do really. I put my fingers in my ears and close my eyes and hide under the red blanket. It is warm and smells of Poddy's fur. 'La, la, la, la,' I say loudly to hide from the sound of guns outside. I giggle because my fingers make my ears tickle. I do all this la la-ing and tickling and laughing and I forget about the guns until Poddy barks urgently and pulls the blanket away with his teeth.

'Woof!' he says seriously.

'No! I won't go!' I say.

'Woof, woof!'

'Poddy, I can't go out there I might get deaded!' The guns are loud and frightnin', and I hide back under the blanket and cry and cry.

Poddy's my best friend. He licks the tears off my cheeks. It makes me laugh again because his pink tongue is rough. It feels funny.

'Woof!' he says again.

'No, Poddy, I won't go!' He growls at me and shows his teeth.

'Stop it!' I say. 'I don't like it when you growl.' And he stops 'cos he loves me.

'You're fierce like a big wolf,' I say. He says I could be fierce too and we do mean faces at each other and giggle. I love Poddy; he makes me feel better, makes me bigger than I am. Mummy says I am ninety-four and a half centipedes tall, which is some sort of measurey thingamyjig. That's not big. Where is mummy?

'I'm not big enough to go out there!' I shout because I know Poddy will make me.

I hear the guns firing again and Poddy reminds me that I am a cowboy and I have two guns of my own. When you make this shape with your hands they make the brilliantest guns. Dad's got them too; he says thumbs are triggers. I fire my guns from the window, leaving sticky prints on the glass.

When Poddy makes me leave the car, both guns are loaded and I'm a cowboy with a snarling dog at his side.

'Peeyow! Peeyow!'

The nasty giant wears an unusual hat. It is black and wide and looks silly on his head. He is still scary though, like a grizzly bear. He is almost as tall as the trees around him. I can't see his face; his back is to me. But he turns quickly when he hears Poddy barking and snarling. He aims the long gun at me! I hate baddies, so I fire both of mine quickly. Peeyow, peeyow!

When the giant falls his eyes are wide like an owl in the night and I have to move because his body is so big and I don't want to be squashed like an ant. I don't like ants and I don't like the body, as it lays there deaded and still among broken twigs and stones. I close my eyes.

When I open them, Poddy is sitting on the giant. He barks a happy bark and has a waggy tail. *'Goodies always win,' he says.*

Daddy says I'm a goodie.

A Fox's Tale

'*For dust you are and to dust you will return.*' **Genesis 3:19**

***

There's a stillness in the air, it feels like time has stopped.

The bird in the sky had elliptical wings. I followed it closely until I reached a copse of trees on a hill. Then it disappeared into a cloudy expanse. Now I sit in the undergrowth amongst the tangle of thorns, my orange fur brushing against blackberries and crisp green foliage. I smell the scent of the wounded boy as he lays next to the bunker, one hand on the cold concrete, the other clutching a pine cone. His grip is tight so I know he lives. I watch the flight of a butterfly; the random movement of its wings: flutter-stop, flutter-stop. It is red and black and white. It rests on the boy's leg, bathing in the remaining warmth of the sun. Sometimes I eat butterflies; they taste of sunshine.

I crouch behind the tree now because I sense the people are coming; my hazel eyes watching, my bushy tail curled around the greying bark of a fallen tree. I crouch. I wait.

The girl with pink hair is lost in the woods behind me, she is exhausted and hungry and her voice is hoarse from shouting. She keeps vomiting but her stomach is empty. She wretches on bile and sobs alternately.

'Amelia! Amelia! Amelia!' she shouts, over and over.

I watched her sink to her knees, flat hands covering her eyes. I sense the depth of her pain; her deep loneliness; it exudes from her every pore. Does she not know that the man with no name is searching for her?

'You are not alone!' I want to shout. But I yelp and whimper and turn my tail and distance myself because her pain hurts me. And now I crouch by the tree, waiting. Death is coming and it wears a wide-brimmed hat.

The tall man who reaches the bunker first is dressed smartly and flanked by the girl with the floaty pony tail and the Priest. They call the tall man *Mr Prime Minister*, and speak with hurried breath. Like the farmer, they carry guns with intent. The large black car ascending the hill smells of rubber and diesel, like the yellow tractor in the barn with the leaky roof. I used to visit the farmer's barn every spring and eat his chickens; they were fed on corn and tasted good, that's why I remember it.

Behind the car a storm lurks in the distance, I can taste the rain from it; it sits in the air expectantly but remains far off. When the car door opens the shadow that emerges is gigantic. It fires bullets rapidly from a long-barrelled gun, and the Priest falls to the floor with a shot to the head and chest.

The boy with the pine cone was crawling through the bracken into the undergrowth and has now disappeared. The girl with the floaty pony tail crouches in front of the tall man, pushing him to the floor. I see the fabric of his suit become snagged and muddy as he crawls tight to the ground. The girl fires bullet after bullet at the man with the long barrelled gun as he vacates the car. But he appears invincible. I see confidence and death in his eyes and I cower in the tree line. Am I too close? My greying fur stands on end as I lie tight to the floor. I am frozen by fear but bound by curiosity. Although I am afraid I do not run because who else will remain to witness these events. Who will tell this story, if not I, the Stranded Fox?

Close to the ground I hear the entry of rushing feet as the girl with pink hair stumbles through the trees. 'Amelia!' she screams. The long-barrelled gun fires instinctively and I am certain she will be dead. But time flickers, as does the light. And the man with no name appears from nowhere. As he dives, the bullet meant for her hits his shoulder and their bodies become one as they hit the wooded floor and lie in the undergrowth. Casually aimed bullets zip overhead.

The girl with the pony tail is shot three times before she dies. She has done her duty: the tall man has escaped and is sealed in the bunker. Her final thought was whether her father would be proud, whether he would be pleased with her sacrifice. She thinks of the Fox Club and I wonder what this is; I am a fox and I have never heard of it.

A little girl jumps from the car into the silent aftermath of the battle. She has rosy cheeks and spies me through the trees with slitted, cat-like eyes.

'A fox!' I hear her whisper.

What is she doing?! *Run little girl! Run away!* I want to shout. Time flickers as does the light of the sun through the canopy of leaves, and in slow motion I watch the dust particles glittering in the air. I close my eyes for what seems like the briefest of moments because I do not want to watch the little girl die.

When I open them the giant lies on the wooded floor and for certain I know his soul has departed and he is no different from the dust beneath him.

Dust. Without God's breath, everything is dust.

I take my leave. And as I go I hear a dog bark.

Assassin (3)

~e᷒᷑~

'For the wages of sin is death.' **Romans 6:23**

***

The air is still and I wish time had stopped. Today is my birthday. I am forty.

My heart beats rapidly as my final bullet enters the artery in Fontaine's neck and I watch her grab at the remains of her life with futility, as she slumps to the ground in a bloody mess. The thief with pink hair and the man with no name are inconsequential now; Develaire has the memory card. They are no longer a threat so I fire at them absently through the trees and remove them from my mind. All that remains is to put a bullet in the head of the Prime Minister and my task is complete. I watched him crawl in the bunker; the most powerful man in the country brought to his knees by a handful of bullets.

As I reload I bathe in the silence; the still aftermath of the gunfight. The birds are quiet, even the leaves do not rustle, all wind has ceased. Fontaine put up a good fight; she was a worthy opponent. But there is only one winner in this game.

'Peeyow, peeyow!'

The sudden noise out of the silence startles me and I spin around to see a little girl with bunches and rosy cheeks standing before me. Where did she come from? There is an innocence about her face. For some reason I am reminded of Hope in the hospital. I recall wiping the streaked mascara from her cheeks; the feel of her hand, the way her fingers locked with mine.

The little girl's fingers are small and pink and point at me in mock gun shapes. Her eyes are thin, like a cat as she attempts a frown.

'Peeyow, peeyow!'

I smile and clutch at my heart, feigning death from imaginary bullets. But beneath my hand I feel an erratic beat, slow then fast. Then even faster; it speeds up and up and up, and the pain is excruciating and as real as the gun that falls from my hand. I double over. And my heart beats and beats and beats. Then nothing. And the last thought going through my mind is that today is my birthday and in all these years no one has ever baked me a cake. The blood stops pumping; the oxygen does not reach my brain and I lose all coherent thought. I fall to the ground amongst twigs and a scurrying of ants as my heart finally stops.

My soul is collected by a ship that has ice in the rigging. The moon is bright and clear. It shines through frozen droplets that hang from the rope like glittering diamonds around a woman's neck. The icy fog that descends upon me is cold and devoid of all light as I slip into the impending silence that is my death. And from the echoes of what was my life, I hear a dog bark.

Still. All is still.   For me

time   has

stopp
    e

      d.

The Letter

———— ୧.୨ ————

I am certain Elisabeth Fontaine is dead when the gunfire stops and I wonder how much time I have before the hitman outside figures how to break into this bunker. I brush off my suit with sore hands and walk down a dark corridor and enter a large room that is illuminated by the soft glow of an emergency lamp. I nearly jump out of my skin at the sight of a pale-looking teenager sitting in a black leather chair.

'Who the hell are you?' I say.

'Can you speak up, I can't hear,' he shouts. It's then that I notice the dried blood down his ears.

'Who are you?' I shout.

'Danny Blackwood.'

'What are you doing here? Are you with Fontaine? Are you part of the Fox Club?'

'Fox Club? No. I came with my grandad.'

'Is he part of the Fox Club? Where is he?'

'I don't know. He had a map that brought us here.'

'A map!?'

'Yeah. It was in a trunk in the loft with a luger and a Nazi flag.'

I'm not sure how to respond so I say, 'Why can't you hear properly, Blackwood?'

'I tripped a wire; there was an explosion.'

'Do you need any medical help? Maybe there's a first aid kit down here.'

'I've looked, the place is empty. There's no phone signal either.'

The boy stares long at me like he wants to say something else.

'Yes, I'm the Prime Minister,' I say as if to answer his unspoken question.

'I know,' he says, frowning, 'you've got mud on your face.'

The boy took the wind out my sails.

'Who are you running from?' he says, making eyes at the door and steps we entered through.'

'That man. The gun,' I say, not sure where he was going with this.

'Is that all?'

'What do you mean, is that all?' I say sharply.

'I've seen you on TV. You never look that confident. The words always sound right, it's just . . . '

'Just what?' I say, irritated.

'Just sounds like its somebody else's speech.' I feel anger rising in the back of my throat.

'Bloody cheek! How old are you?'

'Seventeen.'

'Seventeen!'

'Sorry, I'm just saying what I see.'

There's a long silence; I ponder his words. He watches me in the still space between us. I feel his gaze but I don't look him in the eye. His words cut me. They were harsh but not spoken maliciously. I think of the en-suite at home and the large mirror above the sink; I think of how I wait for the hot steam of the shower to fog it up so I don't have to look that stranger in the eye; his reflection disappoints me. And I wonder whether it would be easier to face the bullet of an assassin's gun than to hear these words from a boy that is not yet a man. These words anger me because I hear the truth in them.

Five minutes later I say: 'What do you mean, sounds like somebody else's speech?'

'I don't know, I guess. . . there's a difference between knowing your path and walking it.'

I look at the pale boy, with messy hair and a bloody face. He looks frail and close to death but his eyes are strong; alert. The profundity of his words have shocked me and I wonder what ever happened to my seventeen-year-old self.

'Have you thought of pursuing politics?' I say.

'No, sir,' he says.

We sat in our own thoughts. I closed my eyes trying to find a solution to the mess I was in but the truth was that I didn't know what to do. There was a gunman outside, my official security detail were protecting someone who looked like me but wasn't me, all the members of the Fox Club that I knew were dead and I was trapped on the inside of the bunker where phones were inoperable.

'How long have we been sitting here?' Danny said finally.

'Five minutes, an hour, who knows?'

'What is this place anyway?'

I was beginning to question that myself but I said: 'A place of safety. A holding position.'

'But there's nothing in here accept that letter,' he says, pointing to a brown envelope propped up on a dusty keyboard.

He was right. There was nothing much except metal filing cabinets. When I looked through them they were empty – faded cardboard pockets but no documents. There wasn't even paper and a pen. No obvious communications. A couple of screens, thick with dust, sat on a long desk but there was no apparent power. I walked up to the envelope and read the handwritten ink. *Mr Prime Minister.*

The paper inside the envelope is heavy and expensive, layered with a distant aroma of cigar smoke. I sense the enormity of the words before I begin to read it.

Dear Mr Prime Minister,

If you are reading this I suspect you are in a spot of bother. Which may mean you are a fool or truly in dire need of help. I hope it is the latter. I do not believe the Fox Club would have brought you here had you not the potential to serve, as every leader should.

Do you believe in destiny? I do. Sometimes it is put upon a man or woman or nation to do something great, something beyond itself. A calling that to ignore would go against the very fabric of your being. I had this calling; all do to a greater or lesser extent. When I was sixteen God gave me a vision of a future. My destiny was to command the defences of London against some terrible foe. It sounds arrogant when spoken aloud, but the vision was so clear I pursued it with a tenacity that nearly got me killed on several occasions; more than I dare to count. I was desperate to inherit this vision; to press my stamp upon the world. I had to wait, and wait I did.

Waiting. One is not much good at waiting in the excitement of youth and early adulthood. I threw myself into military danger and political debate throughout my young life, waiting for my vision to be fulfilled. I was scared of it, but it had a grip on me so tight and wouldn't let go. But I learnt that God's timing is nothing like mans'. Through sheer will and adventurous spirit I rose to the dizzy heights of public acclaim. I was held there momentarily and then dropped from a great height. In my own strength it was not my time. I never gave up because this vision was imprinted upon me. When it finally caught up with me I was an old man by the world's standards. Thirty-three years later we were fighting for our lives in the Battle of Britain. A battle I would not wish upon any nation but an experience I would never forsake. Sadly it is trials that shape you.

God had shaped my character and I went into the war knowing with certainty that we would have victory, but I was never complacent!

Sadly we will always need the War Office. There will always be times when words uttered in peace and diplomacy are no longer heard, and the only means to disperse a vicious opponent is the threat of force.

The days and months ahead were very great and very terrible. The violence of war shows a man for who he is. I did command the defences of London but I did not do it alone. I could not do it alone then or in the days that followed May 8th 1945. The post war months and years were difficult even from the view of the Opposition. It takes much to rebuild a country, to rebuild broken lives.

You cannot do anything truly great alone and the simplest of things are best carried out with company. It's a necessity to be surrounded by good people. Men of integrity, who can fight beside you, keep you grounded. Men who have the guts to tell you when you are wrong. History will not tell you this but my closest confidants were Edward Pritchard and William Blackwood. They were men of purpose, men with conviction and calling. Men who were transparent; not motivated by the need for power.

Mr Prime Minister, pursue your calling and surround yourself with people who won't lie to you. Never give up and God will put upon you the purposes of his heart.

Be a man of courage. Be strong.

Winston Churchill

'Who's it from?' Danny says from over my shoulder.
'Winston Churchill,' I say.
'Churchill?'
'Yes.'
'My grandfather knew Churchill.'
'Did he?'
'Yes sir, I think they may have been great friends.'
I hear the grinding of metal as the thick door opens and white sunlight floods in and blinds me. I am prepared to take a bullet but Blackwood steps in front of me, shielding me with his slight frame. But there are no bullets, just words as a hoarse voice calls from the light.
'Are you OK down there?'
'Who is this?' I shout at the silhouette that stands firm in the doorway. There's a long pause and I sense him thinking.
'My name . . . my name escapes me.'

Listening

I am ordinary. I do not believe you could pick me out of a crowd if you had met me twice. I have learnt that some people are like that; they don't have presence; they are not loud or brash, they don't have endless conversation or continual witty quips that jolt you into spontaneous laughter. The quietness that consumes ordinary people hides beneath hair of unknown colour and eyes of a non-descript shade. The depths of the ordinary man can be discovered when you step inside his circle; the rich gold leaves of their personality lay hidden beneath the acres of crispy brown ones. Leaves revealed when the wind blows strongly.

The odd thing about being ordinary is that one day life catches up and slams into you. It overtakes, and you crash into the extraordinary and drown in the uncertainty, trying desperately to hold on to broken pieces that float near the surface. Mark my words: life has a way of shaking you, so you better be ready.

I was not ready the day of the crash, so I ran. I escaped on two feet and buried the horror of twisted bodies and lives ever changed inside my subconscious. My tongue was silenced, all memory gone until all the broken pieces were washed away or at least hidden in some difficult to reach alcove of the mind. All that remained in the emptiness and silence was the girl and the cold stone walls of the vestry.

I was always a good listener. You have to be when your voice is gone.

When I was a young boy I had recurring nightmares of faceless men with sharpened blades, chasing me. After the fear, all that remained was silence. The images conjured in my mind tormented me. Fear has many guises. My father didn't know what to do. A man of faith, he held my hand at night while I cried in the darkness.

'God's Word is best spoken out loud,' he said one day. And the words he spoke I repeated quietly on wet, salty lips. *The battle is not yours but God's.* Even now when fear returns to cripple me I speak these words out and feel the comfort of knowing that I am not alone.

By the time my voice returned I had learned how to listen. When you really listen to someone it is surprising what you hear. To really listen is hard. You have to give of yourself completely and discard the cascade of images that continually drop into your mind. You have to remove thoughts of what you are doing in half an hour, an hour, tomorrow. Listening is not about you. It is undivided attention; not diluted by thinking of what you want to say. For me this was easy; when your voice is gone and memory suppressed, all that remains is silence.

As I grew up my default position when scared was silence. I was silent when the girl with pink hair found me. She had many words and I listened to every one of them. She never actually told me what happened but I pieced her story together from the words she left out. When she spoke I watched her face, I watched her lips move and form vowels and consonants. I looked into her eyes and saw myself: it was like a mirror reflecting back at me.

She never talked about her family but she talked about her friends, Penny and Stephen and their beautiful little girl, Amelia. She described her intricately, every feature, every laugh and smile. In my mind's eye I could see her in the park, running through leaves. I could hear her high-pitched laugh; see her eyes sparkle as she chased squirrels up trees. She talked about Amelia's grazed knee and how Penny held her when she cried. Tightly like *this*, she said, and pulled her arms close to her body. That was the only time I saw her cry.

'Did you have a child?' I want to say, but the thought remains in my head as silence consumes me.

Much time has travelled by since I first met Samantha J that day in the church. Many things have happened and my memory returned gradually, as did my voice. It is odd but even now I have spoken only a handful of words to her; so now as I sit behind the glass I wait for her nervously.

When we first met we would walk from the church to the café and sit opposite each other, waiting to be served. Her table of choice was in the corner. Quick access to the door, she once said, laughing, but I could tell she was serious. Mugs with hot tea would sit on a green checked table cloth and she would spoon in three sugars and stir clockwise. I could tell she was counting in her head. Counting seconds? Often a miniature milk bottle with a red carnation sat between us. This was all that separated us, and her words would pour out like a stream of water waiting to be released. The torrent of words would cease if a waiter stood too close; then her lips sealed shut. I think my silence helped her.

'You're my rock,' she said one day, and touched my hand. I won't forget that touch. She didn't realise it but she was my anchor, holding me into reality before I was consumed by the ferocity of the oncoming tide.

Each day I wait, hoping that she will come. I wait and wait then wait some more. Much time passes. Then one day, when hope is stretched out and thin, she comes.

I wait for her behind this glass. The glass separates. When she enters I feel my heart beat faster. She is my mirror. Beyond my reflection I see her face and her eyes smile.

I have longed to see these eyes again, because in them, I see as far as I can go.

Amelia and Me

The day after the gunfight I am allowed to visit Amelia. The social worker brings her to a park near Stephen and Penny's house. The park is grand, with acres of green grass dotted with trees and quiet places to sit on wooden benches. Benches with tarnished names; plaques donated for people long dead. I see gold coloured finches chattering overhead and hear the peeling of a church bell, beyond a grey stone wall. I find Amelia's red wellies at the bottom of a yellow slide. She sits at the top, gazing at the clouds with clear blue eyes.

'Amelia,' I say nervously. She looks at me with curiosity, with one eye on the cookies in the plastic box under my arm.

'You've got pink hair,' she says.

'Yes, I have. I like your bunches – they're so pretty.'

She looks up in the air thoughtfully. 'I'm going to have pink hair when I grow up. Did your mummy let you have pink hair when you was little?'

'I haven't got a mummy,' I say.

She's quiet for a bit, then says, 'I haven't got a mummy either. Not anymore.'

'I'm sorry, Amelia.'

'It's OK, I've got Poddy.' She points over to a patch of empty grass. 'He's my best friend and says everything will be alright.'

'Oh,' I say, but she can hear the unbelief in my voice. I can't see Poddy, but this is what I do see:

Green grass
White daisy petals
A dandelion seed floating in the air
Bright sunlight
Amelia's face
Amelia

'Poddy says you are not supposed to see him. Do you have a best friend?' she says.

'Yes.'

'What's your best friend like?'

And I ponder and think. He is strong and calm and quiet.

'He is my rock,' I whisper.

'Are you a princess?' she says, 'Princesses smell of perfume and you smell nice.'

'I'm not a princess, I'm ordinary.'

'Poddy says no one is ordinary.'

'Does he?'

'What's your name?'

'Samantha.'

'Samantha, I collect woodlices and Poddy says there's some over here.' And she points to the grey stone wall and skips towards it, still talking. I love listening to her voice. I follow. 'Do you collect anything?' She's not looking at me; her eyes are scanning the cracks for movement.

'I collect leaves,' I say.

'Leaves,' she says, 'why?'

'I like the look of them; they're all different, even the ones from the same tree. Different sizes and colours. Some have caterpillar holes. Some smell nice.' I watch her thinking about it.

'Will you show me your leaves?'

'I would love that.' And my eyes well up because I have dreamt of this moment for so long. Amelia sneezes twice into her hand and laughs, then slips her now sticky fingers into mine and looks at me tenderly as the tears roll down my cheeks.

'Don't cry, Samantha, Poddy says you're like a shining star, bright on a cold night.'

Between the Glass

❧

When she enters I hear my heart beat faster; I feel it.

Samantha's hair is still pink but she wears it up. It's a small change but it gives her a confident air that she never possessed before.

Left foot first, she steps over the threshold, careful not to touch it with red sneakered feet. Her eyes are wary of the police guard until she sees me and smiles. My heart beats faster; I felt nervous about seeing her. What if she wouldn't come, appalled by what I had done? Stephen and Penny were dead. I thought about the car crash often, it circled in my mind continually now that my memory was complete. Many times in the darkness of my cell, Develaire's accusatory words would play over and over in my mind. I couldn't sleep. What if Samantha hated me?

But here she was. Her eyes were the same, the way they looked at me. And her smile was warm. She came up to the glass.

'Hey,' she said.

'Hey,' I replied nervously. Why was I so nervous? I had seen her every day for weeks. She was my best friend.

'Your voice is deeper than I thought it would be.'

'Is it?'

'Yes.' We gaze at each other and I wish the glass wasn't there because I want to touch her. She laughs and I wonder if she has read my mind.

'How is your shoulder?' she says, looking at the sling.

'It hurts, mainly at night. How's Amelia?' Her face lights up and I relax as the words gush out of her.

'She's amazing. They are going to let me keep her! The social worker is finding us somewhere to live. She's so beautiful. I've taken some photos of her in the park. She loves my collection of leaves . . . ' I watch her lips move as she speaks, and the lines that crease on her face as she smiles. I listen. I look at my gold cross that sits on her neck. The freckled skin of her neck line. I listen to her words and her voice. I see her imperfections and they are beautiful to me. She talks, I listen. And I listen and listen and listen because although there is sorrow in her life, joy filters through.

She finally draws breath and says: 'Tell me something. Something about you. I hardly know anything about you.' I pause, not sure what I should say. And then.

'I'm related to Winston Churchill… and a Nazi Colonel,' I finally answer. It sounds stupid in my ears but it is the truth and I think about it a lot and want to tell her. The weight of history sits heavy upon me.

'A Nazi Colonel?' And I tell her my story, and I know it will be the first of all my stories and she listens and watches my lips move, forming every vowel and consonant. When I finish she clarifies every detail and I know I have waited for her all my life.

When visiting time is over we look at each other through dirty glass that separates. Samantha touches the pane with gloveless hand.

'It's dark in here Samantha. Really dark.'

'It won't be for long. You'll be free again.'

'Will you come back tomorrow?' I say it quickly and hear the urgency in my voice.

'Tomorrow, and the next day,' she says, 'I will come every day.'

And she did. She was in all my tomorrows.

An Epilogue

I AM outside of time.

For you time is linear. I travel through it at the speed of light. Sometimes I stop time and look at the perfection of creation in all directions, to count every dust particle, enjoy every colour; smell every scent. Sometimes I stop time because the pain of looking seems too much for me. Your capacity to hurt each other suffers me much.

I know what you are made of. I know what you are capable of doing. The pain you can cause. You too are capable of great love, sacrificial love that is so deep that I choose to watch it again and again.

I do not have favourites but the man with no name I knew before he was born, before his mother named him. I saw his life unfold in an instant. Seventy-three years gone past in the blinking of an eye. I played it back in slow motion. He was flawed but he was a man after my own heart. I sent him Samantha Just. Without her he would have slipped into oblivion. A life unfulfilled; devoid of purpose.

Right now he sits in his cell, anxious and exhausted, holding on to the love he sees in Samantha's eyes. Guilt sits heavily on his heart for his actions killed Penny and Stephen. The enemy taunts him but I will give him rest for he is truly sorry; it exudes from the very depths of him. When he is older he will learn that he can't earn his redemption. There is only grace.

Tonight. In the middle of the night. I will wake him. He will remember a verse his father taught him. *A cord of three strands is not quickly broken.* I whispered it to Solomon many years earlier and he recorded it in my Book. He was flawed too, but asked for wisdom. And I gave it because the wisdom wasn't for him, it was for others.

When he wakes and remembers and speaks it out loud, I will

whisper: *You are one of these strands.* And he will know his purpose because I will paint it for him in a dream. Within a year he will walk into a Peace Conference. Daniel Blackwood and the Prime Minister will be beside him and together they will change the course of history forever. How is this possible you ask; nothing is impossible with God. I AM.

I know you are thinking of Amelia. There is much I can say about Amelia. Everyone could be innocent like her. I could tell you her complete story and it would put a smile on your face that would stay there for days. But for you, at this point in time, her story is not yet written. So you can wait; much of life's beauty is in the waiting.

I love you. In the darkness I will still love you and I will pull you out.

All have a choice. Choose wisely.

Author's Note

—◦◦—

Some people will read this and say I have put too much of God and the Bible in this work; others will read it and say, not enough. I just know that when I write I feel God's pleasure.

I follow Jesus. You may laugh or mock me but my freedom is complete.

Author's Note (2)

Although there are elements of truth surrounding the detail of the stories in *Stranded Foxes* that feature Winston Churchill, Ernest Hemingway and Robert Capa, this is essentially a work of fiction and is not an accurate account of their lives or speech.

However, there is truth in Winston Churchill's calling and he really did have a vision of his future as a 16 year-old boy. I would recommend reading *God and Churchill*, authored by Jonathan Sandys and Wallace Henley.

Ernest 'Papa' Hemingway and the war photographer, Robert Capa were great friends and lived intensely interesting lives – anyone wishing to research the stories behind Hemingway's 'Liberation of Paris' and Capa's famous photographs of the invasion of Normandy on 6th June 1944, would not be disappointed!

My prayer is that you would not let the opportunity of reading further around the Biblical verses pass you by. Mark's Gospel is exceptionally well written and confirms the good news about the son of God, Jesus, and offers salvation for *everybody* through His grace.

Bibleography

⌒ᴗᴗ⌒

Between the Glass   Romans 12: 10
An Epilogue   Exodus 3: 14
                                     Ecclesiastes 4: 12